Cover design by Mark Pate

Readers are encouraged to go to www.MissionPointPress.com to
contact the author or to find information on how to buy
this book in bulk at a discounted rate.

Published by Mission Point Press
2554 Chandler Rd.
Traverse City, MI 49696
(231) 421-9513
www.MissionPointPress.com

ISBN: 978-1-950659-71-5
Library of Congress Control Number: 2020914992

Printed in the United States of America

Marietta Hamady

Mission Point Press

*Dedicated with love to my husband,
Ralph Hamady, whose unwavering
support throughout life helped make
my dreams come true.*

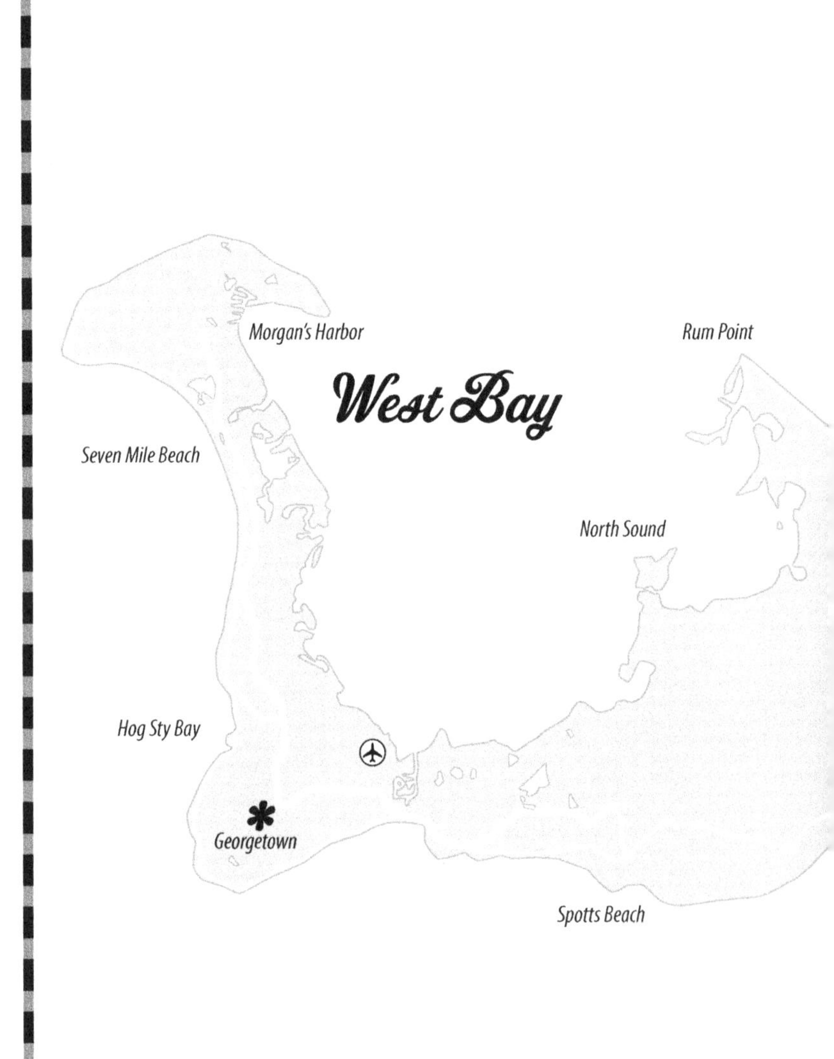
Morgan's Harbor
Rum Point
West Bay
Seven Mile Beach
North Sound
Hog Sty Bay
Georgetown
Spotts Beach

Grand Cayman

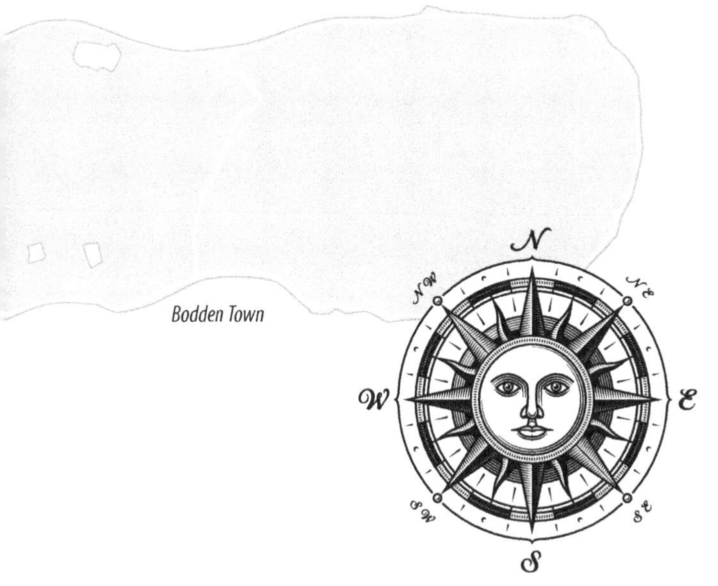

– 1 –

Jilted Jack Goes on Vacation

Struggling up from the beach chair, Jack frowned at the unfamiliar aches and pains in his thirty-two-year-old body. *Broken heart, broken-down body.* He'd hoped the combination of Caribbean sun plus gin and tonics would serve as the balm he sought for his tattered psyche. He gazed out at the ocean, transfixed by the calming repetition of small waves breaking on the shore and retreating, the white froth a contrast to the vivid lapis blue of the deeper water.

His flight landed at Grand Cayman's Owen Roberts Airport around noon. Shortly after, a taxi dropped him off at the Sandy Beach Resort. He hastily unpacked and lay stretched out on a beach chair for the rest of the afternoon, sipping drinks and trying to read a Stephen King thriller. To anyone passing by, he would appear to be the postcard of contentment. But behind the sunglasses, his mind's eye reviewed scenes of his almost-wedding. Images flashed through his brain like an old-school slide show presentation. *Click,* the guests neatly arranged on the church pews. *Click,* his happy, smiling parents. *Click,* his best man, offering him a last-minute nip of bourbon from a silver flask.

Reliving the intense emotions of that day—his anticipation to see Rachel waiting for him at the altar—was the final straw. He fought the lump in his throat and turned to gather up his beach paraphernalia. He hesitated, and then opened the little cooler nestled in the sand next to his chair. *What the hell. One more drink. More ice, more gin—fuck the tonic.* He scooped some slushy ice into his sand-speckled plastic cup, followed by a generous slosh of liquor.

Beach towel around his neck, drink in hand, Jack glanced at the horizon one last time. A peachy-pink sky complemented the sinking sun, now just mere inches from disappearing. He rose, collecting his cooler, turned and trudged through the sand toward his condo and a shower. Along the way, couples drifted toward the beach to salute the day's end, cocktails in hand. A sharp reminder of his single status.

He took a healthy swig of his drink and grimaced as sand from the cup's rim coated his bottom lip. Sticky from sunscreen, hot, irritable and buzzed, he reached the sidewalk leading to his condo and emptied the drink into a bougainvillea bush. The same round of questions that had already tortured him a thousand times that day poked through the gin haze. *What did I do wrong? Why did she run?*

He heaved another sigh as he unlocked the door to his condo. No other prospects for the evening, so he opted for dinner for one at the beach bar next door.

Dining alone was an abysmal experience, the fish tacos barely registering with his taste buds. Jack cruised through a few martinis, staggered back to his condo by way of the beach, and flopped into bed around ten. Sometime later, he awoke with a full bladder and a headache. He wandered into the bathroom, peed, and scrounged around for a couple of aspirin from his Dopp kit. He swallowed them with a gulp of desalinated water from the tap, grimacing at the taste.

On the way back to bed, a misty breeze dampened his skin. He shivered and crawled beneath the soft cotton sheet. The digital clock read 2:01. The window's filmy curtain billowed into the room, and the shirt he'd earlier tossed over the wicker chair fell to the floor. He detected—he was sure of it—a faint odor of burning pipe tobacco. Returning to sleep was his top priority, but he remembered opting for the air conditioning in favor of an open window. *So, why do I smell pipe smoke—and why are the curtains flapping in the breeze?*

Curious, he partially sat up and stared at the window. *Investigate? Or go back to sleep?* His brain nagged him to choose sleep. As he began to sink back under the covers, a swirling mist seeped from the window into the room, followed by a loud clap of thunder.

Jack jerked upright and squinted, trying to make sense of it all. The haze drifted from corner-to-corner like it was assessing the room. He resisted the temptation to rub his eyes, afraid he'd somehow erase the strange scene before him. The possibility of being pinned beneath the sheet made him get out of bed, skin prickling, all senses alert. The thunder rumbled again, causing the lampshade on the bedside stand to rattle. The wispy mass settled at the foot of the bed.

"What the hell are you?" asked Jack.

The only response was a soft sound, like mocking laughter. The apparition vanished. The curtains hung straight, undisturbed. Jack glanced at the clock—still 2:01. Mere seconds had passed.

– 2 –

Jack Runs into a Beach Bar

Darkness gradually surrendered to daylight, and sunshine invaded Jack's bedroom, coaxing him from a deep slumber. He stretched, enjoying the first few glorious seconds of wakefulness—that peaceful period of suspended time. And then, in a flash, reality crashed into his conscious mind like an overloaded semi. Groaning, he rolled over and thought of Rachel. The worst part? He had no closure on the whole mess. Hadn't seen or talked to her, in spite of various attempts, since she'd jilted him three months ago. Rachel faded into the background, replaced by the memory of the swirling mist from the night before.

"What the hell *was* that? I must be losing my mind. Too much gin, too many martinis. And now I'm talking to myself."

He got up, pulled on a tee shirt and shorts and inspected the closed bedroom window. The lever appeared to be in the locked position, but he fiddled with the mechanism to make sure. Satisfied, he shook his head, mystified at why the curtains had billowed into the room during the wee hours. *And what about that thunder-sound?* He headed for the kitchen and coffee.

Minutes later, steaming mug in hand, Jack opened the sliding glass door to a screened porch bathed in sunlight. The warm and humid sea-scented air commingled with the aroma of freshly cut grass. He soaked up the summer-like environment, grateful to be on vacation. An ambitious team of landscape workers swarmed the grounds, mowing the dense zoysia grass and trimming the tropical plants. Jack recognized some of the varieties, but in Michigan they were houseplants. Here, they grew in the ground and were Jurassic Park-sized, thanks to an endless growing season.

One man, dressed in khaki work clothes and armed with a hand saw, deftly climbed a palm tree with nothing more than a braided leather strap wrapped around himself and the tree. He hitched himself up the trunk one step at a time, repositioning the strap as he ascended. The man disappeared from view among the foliage, and soon the brown, dead palm fronds fell to the ground as he sawed through their tough, wiry fibers. Jack judged the fronds to be at least six feet long. Dreary Michigan seemed light years away.

He'd just settled into his chair when he heard a knock at the front door. *Now what?* Irritated, he frowned, marched to the door and flung it open. Facing him stood a young woman holding a clipboard. Jack put his attitude on hold, smoothed out his frown, and observed. Dark, animated eyes with a hint of amusement met his gaze. Her coppery-brown skin provided a pleasing contrast to a shell-pink sleeveless dress. A ring of keys hung on her wrist. He stepped back, embarrassed at showing his impatience.

She flashed a bright smile. "Good morning. I hope I'm not disturbing you, Mr. Garrett."

"Oh, not at all. Call me Jack, and please, come in. You know my name, but yours is . . . ?"

"Of course, sorry." She stepped into the condo. "I'm Jessica Banks, the property manager. I came by to tell you a repairman from the cable company is scheduled to stop by sometime this afternoon. You may have noticed—your cable TV isn't working."

"I didn't notice. Haven't even turned on the TV. But thanks for letting me know."

"Have a good day, Jack."

"Thanks. You too."

The memory of his eerie night was still fresh. Just as she turned to walk away, Jack bit into his lower lip and said, "Um, I'm curious. Did you hear the thunder last night? There was a loud clap, and then some rumbling; even rattled the lamp on my bed stand."

"I didn't hear anything, but I sleep soundly." Jessica furrowed her brows in thought. "Nobody's commented on a storm."

"Oh, no matter. I was probably dreaming."

She laughed. "Too much Caribbean rum?"

"Yeah, maybe that's it." He felt his face heat up. *Is my hangover that obvious?*

"Well, enjoy your day," she said. Jack watched her walk away, admiring her wavy hair bouncing around her shoulders, noting her trim figure and rounded little behind. She turned a corner. *Shouldn't stare at other women. Wait—I can stare. Not engaged anymore.* A bittersweet realization hit him. *My first step toward healing.*

A contented feeling caught him by surprise as he closed the door. The unscheduled day stretched before him, and he decided to walk off the martini indulgence from the night before. A few yards away from his door, the most beautiful beach in the Caribbean extended for miles in either direction. Jack slathered sunblock on his winter-white skin, grimacing as he was unable to reach the middle of his back. He sighed. *One of the pitfalls of being alone.*

He strolled the short distance to the beach, kicked off his flip-flops and meandered along the sandy shore. Soon, he relaxed to the sound of the waves as his body responded to the ocean's ancient rhythm, releasing some of his emotional stress. His gaze focused on the water's varied hues, ranging from turquoise to aqua. Breathing in the warm sea air, he felt revitalized, tension melting away in the sunshine.

Maybe exchanging Michigan's frigid winter temperatures for warmth and sun would prove to be the balm for his weary soul. His last look at the Mitten State had been from the plane's window, heavy snow falling helter-skelter through the air.

Memory of the strange events in the early morning hours faded in the dazzling sunlight. Jack vowed to moderate his alcohol intake for the rest of the week. Gin and rum were merely Band-Aids, certainly not the answer to his problems. His gaze shifted. In the distance, he noticed a cluster of people on the beach and in the surf. He picked up the pace and jogged towards the throng.

Strains of calypso and reggae music, along with the aroma of hot grease, wafted from a nearby beach bar. People milled about in the ocean, holding their long-neck beer bottles out of the roiling surf, while others glistened and baked on beach chairs, umbrella drinks in hand.

Tempting as it was to stop and gawk at the people soup, Jack jogged on. The phrase 'The good, the bad, and the ugly' came to mind, and he chuckled to himself. *Airport people-watching has nothing on this scene.* Young hard-bodies, punctuated by tattoos, strutted about in the skimpiest of swimwear. Middle-aged women stubbornly clung to their youth, their jiggly parts stuffed into bikinis, the Lycra fabric stretched beyond factory tolerance. Men, their prime years in the rear-view mirror, sported Speedo briefs, their beer bellies providing shade for the packages they hadn't seen in years.

He jogged past the colorful scene, his thoughts drifting to Rachel in yet another attempt to dissect her behavior on their wedding day. They'd been engaged for three years. *How could she spring a surprise like that on me?* A bolt of anger shot through him, because he knew it wasn't likely he'd ever find out why she did it. Her parents, disgusted by her actions, apologized to Jack and shared their disappointment, but wouldn't tell him where she was as she'd sworn them to secrecy. *Fuck the secrecy; they owe me at least that much.*

After jogging what felt like a couple of miles, Jack paused, breathing heavily, and turned around. He enjoyed the exercise and sweating in the sun, a welcome physical and mental cleanse.

On the return trip, the aromas of grilled and fried food proved impossible to ignore. His hangover needed nourishment, and only the best grease would do. A brightly painted crooked sign poked up from the sand, bearing the name Rum Runners. Jack stopped at the wooden planked bar, noting that the white paint, chipped in all the right places, emitted a homey and inviting vibe. People in vacation mode, some pale, some tanned, perched on bar stools in bathing suits, leaning against the bar and each other, enjoying the first cocktails of the day.

Jack raised his hand, catching the eye of the bartender, who sported an impressive head of dreadlocks. He nodded and called out, "Mornin', man. Runnin' a special on Bloody Marys. Interested?"

"Uh, no thanks," Jack said, his stomach growling. "Got a table for an early lunch?"

He gestured toward a two-top in the shade. "That work for ya?"

"Sure, thanks."

He flopped into the chair, grateful for the large-bladed fan stirring the air above. Only 11:00, and he guessed the temperature to be at least eighty degrees.

A pretty waitress wearing a white floppy beach hat placed a laminated menu on the table and smiled. "Welcome to Rum Runners. Anyone joining you?"

Feeling that familiar twist in his gut, he answered, "Uh, not today."

"All by yourself, eh?" She grinned. "That won't last long."

Jack raised his eyebrows. "Oh?"

She leaned in and said, "It's cruise ship day."

"Okay. What does that mean?"

"Four cruise ships in port today. Rum Runners is a hot spot; a real swingin' place, if you get my drift." She winked as if she'd just gifted him a critical bit of information.

"Good to know. I guess that explains the interesting crowd on the beach."

"Now you're catchin' on. Anything to drink?"

"Bottled beer—any recommendations?"

"Caybrew, a local beer, is popular—a decent lager."

"Okay. I'll have that plus a burger and fries."

"Sure. Be right out." She tossed another wink his way.

What's with all the winking? Is she trying to hit on me? He shook his head at his own cluelessness. *So out of practice.*

Moments later, the cold Caybrew showed up. He poked a lime wedge into the long-neck bottle and brought it to his mouth. Mid-swallow, a bikini-clad woman brandishing an umbrella drink plunked down into the chair across the table from him.

"How 'bout some company?"

Jack stared at the sight before him. Too tan, too tattooed, and too drunk.

"Um, I'm waiting for someone ... sorry."

She produced a soft burp, shook her finger at him, and said in a singsong voice, "Now, now, that's not what you told the waitress. Said you were all alone." She emphatically nodded, causing her boobs to jiggle like coddled ostrich eggs, barely contained within the two-sizes-too-small fringed bikini top. Jack shifted his gaze from the impressive rack to the cat's head tattoo situated just above her cleavage, the inked whiskers expanding the width of her chest.

He had a hard time believing his luck. Jilted at his wedding, and now a magnet for the drunk and desperate.

The waitress delivered his lunch and murmured under her breath, "Can't say I didn't warn you."

He rolled his eyes in response. As tempting as it was to extricate himself from the clutches of Drunk Girl and simply leave, his empty stomach and hungry eyes voted for the burger and fries, plus another beer.

He bit into the hot, juicy sandwich.

"So, whatsh yurname?" She pulled a French clip from the top of her blonde head, fluffed her hair, and repositioned the clip, missing all the hair on one side, which now hung like straw at her shoulder.

"Jack."

"Jaaaack. You're kinda cute. What ship're you on?"

"I'm not on a ship."

She frowned and tilted her head. "You're not a cruiser?"

"Nope."

She tapped the table with a neon-orange lacquered nail and stage-whispered, "My ship leaves at four." Waving her index finger back and forth between the two of them, she added, "Maybe we could hook up, you know, have some fun." She trailed her fingers across her tattooed chest and giggled. "Wanna make my kitty purr?" A lopsided grin accompanied the generous offer.

Jack continued to plow through his lunch. "No, thanks. I'm enga ... I mean, I have to go."

Gazing at his empty plate, she frowned and stuck out her lower lip. "You didn't even save me a fry." Her face brightened, and she raised her eyebrows. "But you can buy me a drink."

With perfect timing, the waitress dropped the bill on the table. Jack grabbed his wallet, removed some cash and made a hasty exit, leaving the tattooed chick trying to suck up the last bit of pink foam in her glass with a kinked straw.

The rest of the day was Caribbean-perfect, and Jack camped out in the shade with his laptop. He checked his work email account, happy to see nothing required his immediate attention. However, the personal emails from friends and family caused him angst. His parents worried about him, and his friends offered cheerful diversions in the form of newsy messages and humor. He appreciated their kindness, but nothing could replace the emptiness in his heart. Not one word from Rachel, keeping him firmly planted in the dark.

– 3 –

Taste of the Caribbean

The sun continued its predictable trek across the sky, signifying the dinner hour fast approaching. Mindful of his greasy lunch, Jack decided a healthier meal was the smart choice.

After he showered and dressed, he thumbed through a local entertainment magazine and discovered Grand Cayman boasted two hundred and forty-three restaurants—on an island only twenty-two miles long and four miles wide. He whittled down the choices and opted for the Sunshine Grill, a highly rated place within walking distance.

After a bit of a search, he realized the little restaurant had no street access but was tucked in the middle of a resort. He sensed a friendly vibe as he walked through the open French doors. A lively bar area and tantalizing aromas told him he'd made the right choice. In here, dining solo wouldn't be so god-awful lonely.

A blonde waitress smiled as she approached him, menu in hand. Her voice was soft, and Jack detected a British accent. "Good evening, welcome to Sunshine Grill. Table for… ?"

Jack gave a rueful smile. *Gotta get used to this question.* "Just one, please."

"Sure. Follow me."

She led him to the choicest table in the place, directly in

front of an open louvered window framing the view of a hibiscus plant, its red flowers bobbing in the breeze.

"My name's Kate. I'll be taking care of you this evening." She placed a spiral-bound booklet in front of him. "Our cocktail menu. The drinks are absolutely brilliant." Opening the cover, she brushed her hand against his arm and tapped on a colorful photo of some tropical concoction, tilted her head, and said, "The piña colada is my favorite."

He smiled. "Give me a minute to check out the menu—oh, and thanks for the recommendation."

He observed her as she left his table. *Was she flirting?* Shaking his head, he sighed.

Intrusive thoughts of Rachel poked their way into his mind, and he caught himself in an unfocused stare. He glanced at the surrounding tables, wondering if he'd inadvertently fixed his gaze on a fellow diner, but no one seemed to be paying any attention to him. Irritation and anger washed over him. *Damn it, Rachel—you threw me into the singles world again, and I hate it!* He squeezed his eyes shut, and stress descended on him like a virus. *I need a fucking drink.* He flipped through the cocktail menu.

The waitress returned with a sparkling smile. "Did you decide?"

"Yes. Um, I'll try a Dark and Stormy." *Matches my mood.*

"Brilliant choice; it's delicious."

"Good to know." A mental image of the drunk and tattooed woman with her foo-foo drink flashed in his mind. "Don't want anything pink and frothy."

"I completely agree. I'll be right back with your Dark and Stormy. Sounds dangerous, doesn't it?"

"I hope not too dangerous—watching myself tonight."

She smiled again, returned shortly with the amber-colored drink, and set it on a coaster in front of him. Halfway through the cocktail, he concluded that the combination of dark rum and Jamaican ginger beer represented the flavors of the Caribbean, prompting him to order the house specialty, Havana Chicken.

When dinner arrived, the spicy aromas made him realize how ravenous he felt. Unlike the previous night's fish tacos, he enjoyed every single bite of the crispy citrus-marinated chicken and local greens salad.

Kate reappeared as Jack finished his last bite. "You simply must have our famous key lime pie. There's no avoiding it."

"I rarely have dessert… but, if it's a must…"

"Absolutely. It's the best on the island. Our pastry chef spreads a thin layer of chocolate ganache between the crust and the filling. Divine!"

"Hard to say no to that cute British accent."

She blushed. "A lot of Brits work on the island. You know that Cayman's a British Territory?"

"I figured that out when I noticed everyone driving on the wrong side of the road."

She tucked her hair behind her ear and laughed. "Oh, you Americans—you mean the *left,* not the wrong side of the road."

Kate came back moments later with an ample slice of pie garnished with a whipped cream swirl and twisted lime slice.

Jack dove into the dessert, and when Kate returned, he said, "You were right. The key lime pie lives up to its hype."

"Thought you might say that." She placed the check on the table.

He handed his credit card to her.

She glanced at the card. "It's been nice chatting with you, ah, Jack Garrett. Um, I'm working during the day tomorrow. You should come back for lunch."

"Maybe I will." Inwardly he grimaced and thought how grueling it'd be to enter the singles world again. *Match.com, here I come.*

Jack ambled back to the condo, wondering if he should return for lunch tomorrow. *What's the point? I live in Michigan and, well, she doesn't.* Weariness settled in behind his eyes. He felt exhausted. Maybe it was all the sunshine and fresh air, or the stress of dipping a toe in the turbulent waters of single life again. Just like the night before, he fell into bed around ten o'clock and entered a deep sleep in record time.

A knock on the wall awakened Jack. He sat up in bed, groggy and confused. The air felt heavy, as if a presence was sucking up all the oxygen. Like before, a wispy substance seeped from the window to settle at the foot of his bed. The ghostly mass began moving like a mini-tornado, last night's encounter paling in comparison to what manifested before him now.

The spinning, abstract shape gradually took on human form. A masculine head emerged, sporting a tri-cornered hat atop long, shaggy black hair. Fierce, dark eyes glared at Jack. A scar ran through an eyebrow and across the bridge of a hooked nose. Chipped and rotted teeth clamped a pipe stem, curls of aromatic smoke rising from its curved bowl. Broad shoulders filled out a stained and blousy white shirt; a belt with a silver buckle cinched ragged breeches tucked into worn leather boots. Completing the image was a cutlass, its hilt secured in the belt, the menacing curved blade dangling exposed at his side.

"What the fuck?" Jack scrambled up from the bed. "Wh-what are you ... ?" The base of his spine tingled, knowing the answer even as he asked the question.

"A ghost, matey."

The apparition seemed so real that Jack stared, searching for signs of actual flesh and bone. He started to reach out to touch the specter, but pulled back his hand abruptly. *Don't wanna get sucked into his world.* Jack hadn't been exposed to ghosts since his childhood, and then only the fictionalized kind. The *Goosebumps* books and *Ghostbusters* movie were his only sources of knowledge of the spirit world. Now here he was, a grown man, in the presence of a fully formed ghost—an undeniable proof of life after death. *Unless I'm just going nuts.*

Jack swallowed. "Who are you?"

The ghost laughed, making his image shake. With an exaggerated gesture, he doffed the hat and held it over his heart. "Me name's Alejandro, th' greatest pirate ever ta sail th' Caribbean."

Jack couldn't decide whether to bolt or freeze. He gauged the distance between the bed and the door, but the pirate's wavy mass blocked his path. *Can I run through a ghost?* Seeing no easy way out, he forced himself to take a couple deep breaths and stay still.

The ghost drifted closer, settling into the wicker chair next to Jack's bed. Acting as if he owned the place, Alejandro stretched out his legs and put his boot-clad feet on the bed. He removed the pipe from his mouth, reached into his pocket, and pulled out a wad of tobacco, tamping it into the bowl. A tiny flame materialized, and the contents appeared to catch fire.

Jack noticed that the chair squeaked and the cushion compressed when the ghost sat down. *What kinda ghost is this? He weighs something.* A feeling of danger rippled through him. However, with the ghost in the chair, Jack realized he now had an escape route. He edged over toward the bedroom door.

Alejandro spoke between puffs. "'Bout time ye woke up. Had to resort to Ghost Tricks 101—knockin' on walls."

With one hand on the doorknob, Jack asked, "You were here last night, weren't you?"

"Aye."

"Why are you here now?"

The transparent intruder didn't answer, just smiled and puffed on his pipe, the fragrant smoke swirling around his head, causing Jack to worry. *What's in that smoke?* He pictured himself sprawled out on the floor, paralyzed, as the ghost did God-knows-what to him.

"Git yer hand off th' doorknob. Yer not goin' anywhere."

Jack turned the knob, ready to make a break for it. The ghost made a gesture, and the knob counter-turned in his hand, leaving the door firmly shut.

"Nothin' ta fear," said the ghost. "Ain't plannin' to hurt ya."

"What do you want?" Jack's heart banged away in his chest. Seeing himself as a victim pissed him off. "Forget it." Scowling, he waved at the hazy air in front of his face. "I don't wanna know. Just leave."

"Or what? Ye gonna slice me inta ribbons with yer sword?" The pirate cupped his ear as if struggling to hear. "What? Ye got no sword?" He barked out a laugh.

Jack frowned. "Fine, I'll ask again. What do you want?"

The ghost's eyes flashed in the darkness. "'Tis not what *me* wants, 'tis what *ye* needs, Jack." He stabbed at the air with a bejeweled finger, emphasizing his point.

"How do you know my name?"

"Alejandro knows all."

"Great. A know-it-all ghost."

Alejandro pointed his pipe stem at Jack. "Ya know ye coulda had 'er."

"Wha … ? What are you talking about?"

"Ar ye daft? Th' tattooed wench at Rum Runners."

Jack shook his head, trying to keep pace with the bizarre situation, amazed he was conversing with a ghost. "How do you even know about that—are you crazy? I wouldn't touch her with a ten-foot pole."

Alejandro chuckled. "Yer the cautious type, ain't ya?"

Jack ignored the comment. He spotted his cell phone on the edge of the dresser and grabbed it. "This is your final warning—get the hell out of here, or I'm calling the cops."

"Ain't so smart, are ye? Disappearin's me specialty. Cops won't find nuthin'."

Jack extended his arms, hands palms up. "So, what does it take to get you to leave me alone?"

"Now we're gettin' somewhere. Negotiatin's me other specialty."

– 4 –

Alejandro's Proposal

"Negotiate? Negotiate what? You're a ghost!"

Alejandro drifted through the closed bedroom door. "Got any grog?"

Jack yanked open the door and hurried after the wispy intruder. He stopped, mouth agape, and watched the refrigerator open. A bottle of beer levitated toward the ghost. "What the... hey, wait a minute—that's my beer."

Alejandro put the bottle to his mouth, pried off the cap, and spit it on the floor. He downed the beer in one long gulp, which splashed to the floor, nary a drop contained in his ghostly body.

"Aaah, ain't grog and ain't rum, but it ain't bad."

Jack pointed at the puddle. "What the hell are you doing? You're makin' a mess—spilling beer all over the place."

Alejandro glanced down, belched and guffawed. "Well, blow me down, can't hold me liquor like th' ol' days."

Jack glared at the unruly ghost. "Are you what's known as a poltergeist, or are you just a pain in the ass?" He scowled, peered out the open kitchen window, shut it, and closed the blinds, now convinced that the ghost was a reality and maybe not leaving anytime soon.

"Who ye lookin' for? That saucy wench, Jessica?" Alejandro pranced around the room, swinging his butt and pulling his shirt away from his chest, mimicking boobs. In a falsetto voice, he said, "Oh, Jaaack, th' cable man's comin' today. Oh, Jaaack, wanna swab me deck?"

Jack whisper-shouted, "Shut up! You're disgusting, and you're too loud with your, your childish antics."

Alejandro zipped across the room to hover in front of Jack. Giving him an appraising look, he nodded and stroked his chin. "Aye, methinks ye need to get laid. Part of yer problem. Yer all stopped up."

"You're full of shit... how do you know what I need?"

The ghost put his hands on his hips. "See? Yer jumpy. *And* yer no fun. Maybe ye ain't th' one."

"What do you mean I'm no fun and 'ain't th' one?' The one what?"

"Ye ask a lot of questions—exactly seven, in only five minutes." He extracted a pocket watch from his vest and squinted. "Aye, only five minutes. C'mon, ya smarmy land lubber, Alejandro's gettin' restless. Time to go wenchin'."

"Wenchin'...yeah, that's a great idea—for you. Now get outta here. It's midnight, and I'm not going anywhere except back to bed."

Jack felt a force at his back, like a driving wind, propelling him toward the front door.

"Stop it! I'm not dressed!"

"Ye better put on yer clothes then."

Jack summoned up his courage, whirled around, and faced the scowling ghost, arms crossed. "No. You'd better start answering some questions. You've gone far enough, and I will *not* let a ghost push me around. So, out with it—why are you here, and why are you bothering me?"

The ghost crossed his arms, imitating Jack's stance, and huffed. "Yer damned nosy. But since ye asked, me notification came through."

"Notification?"

"Aye, from up there." He pointed toward the ceiling.

Jack shrugged. "And?"

Alejandro blinked and averted his gaze. "Got me cross-over orders."

"Cross over to what?"

"To th' other side, ya daft lunatic."

"When?"

"In a few days."

"That's good, isn't it?" Jack's mood brightened at the thought of Alejandro vanishing permanently into the afterlife.

Alejandro stomped his foot. "Damn it! This island's been me home fer three-hundred-and-twenty yar. Had th' run o' th' place—threw out every last scallawaggin' ghost back in '14."

Jack frowned. "2014?"

The ghost shot Jack a withering look. "No. 1714. Been roamin' this patch o' land by meself ever since."

Jack nodded. "So, you've enjoyed exclusive haunting rights, and now you have to give all that up. I understand why you might be pissed off—you'll miss all the fun you've been having for the last three hundred-odd years." He put air quotes around the word 'fun.'

Alejandro's eyes narrowed. "Had more fun than yer scabby arse, sittin' 'round cryin' like a baby over that shark-bait wench, Rachel."

"Shut up about Rachel." He scowled. "How do you even know about her?"

"Alejandro knows all. And, ya talk in yer sleep."

Jack waved his hand in a dismissive manner. "Why should I listen to you? You're not even real." He reached out, attempting to touch the ghost, but his hand moved through air—perhaps just a few degrees cooler. "See? No flesh, no bones. You can't drink, can't eat, can't screw. Yeah, that's one helluva great time, Casper."

The ghost rattled the cutlass at his side. "Show some respect, ya snivelin' worm. Ye'll have a face full o' me boot, if ya don't shut up."

Jack put up his hands. "Fine. Sure, your story pulls at my

heartstrings, but it seems like a one-man problem. Once again, what does it take to get you to leave me alone?"

The ghost rubbed his transparent hands together. "Aye, this is th' negotiatin' part." He held up three fingers. "Be me bucko for three days, and, after that, ye'll never see this screw-eyed pirate agin."

"Your bucko?"

"Aye; me matey. Been knockin' around by meself fer too long—could use a bucko me last few days on this island."

"You mean, be your friend?" Jack frowned and shook his head. "I don't think so—don't need a bucko right now. I'm trying to get my life back in order; I need R&R time. It's best that you leave, find someone else. I'm not *the one*."

The ghost shook a finger at Jack. "Think twice before ye throw me overboard." He poked himself in the chest with his thumb. "Ye need some fun in yer life, and this shaggy bastitch is th' best man fer th' job."

Thoroughly exasperated, Jack ran his fingers through his hair. "Fun? But you're a *ghost*. What would we do? If nobody can see you but me—or wait, can other people see you too?"

The ghost grinned. "Once in a while, somebody'll see this ol' pirate." His face lit up like a lighthouse, happy to trot out another selling point. "Oh, and th' ladies like me." He danced a little jig, licked his pinky and ran it across his scarred eyebrow.

"Ye and me together—th' wenches will be ripe for th' pickin'." Alejandro prattled on, trying to close the deal. "Got me a few tricks, ya know. Ya might learn somethin'." His eyebrows shot up, anticipating an affirmative response.

"Learn something?" Jack scoffed. He shook his head, hearing his father's words summing up his failed relationship as a 'learning experience.' At the time, he'd been annoyed by the insinuation that he had anything left to learn at the age of thirty-two, especially when it came to women. And yet, here were the same words coming from an undead pirate ghost.

He plunked down on the sofa. A memory surfaced of he and Rachel searching for the ideal venue for their wedding reception. They'd visited four hotels, two restaurants, and a country club, and the strongest emotion Rachel had displayed was indifference. *Too stupid to read the clues—how many others did I miss?*

Jack stared at Alejandro, wondering what a night out on the town would be like with a ghost. "You still in a negotiating mood?"

"Aye. What's ye proposin'?"

"We'll hang out for one night and one night only. Then you leave me alone to enjoy the rest of my vacation. Deal?"

The ghostly pirate shot up toward the ceiling and fist-pumped like he'd just found buried treasure. "Deal. Let's go!"

"Oh, no. Not tonight. Tomorrow night—come by at ten."

Alejandro saluted Jack, spun in place until he resembled a small tornado, and then zipped out the window.

Jack closed his eyes. *What in the hell did I just agree to do? Ha—the ultimate Caribbean adventure. A night on the town with a ghost.*

– 5 –

Walkin' th' Plank

Jack's hand hovered over the laptop's keyboard. He'd spent an hour crafting his last email to Rachel, trying to strike the right tone. *Concerned, not angry, questioning but not pushy—blah, blah, blah—walking on eggshells. I'm done trying to second-guess what's going on in her head, and I'm tired of begging her to tell me. Just want some closure.* His index finger tapped "send," and the whooshing sound assured him the email was on its way.

This afternoon, parked under the shade of a palm tree, he'd sifted through the flotsam of his life. A few months ago he'd been pleased with his personal trajectory, and assumed years of contentment stretched before him. Now, doubts picked at his model for happiness. Perhaps he had it all wrong. Maybe he'd been too buttoned-down and predictable; maybe Rachel couldn't abide the thought of a lifetime spent in comfortable mediocrity.

A reminder popped up on the laptop's screen: Alejandro, 10:00. Jack glanced at the time—9:45. He headed to the bedroom, amused at the thought of scheduling a three-hundred-year-old ghost with 21st-century technology. In fact, why did he even set up a reminder? As if he could forget a date with a ghost. On the other hand, at least there'd be a cyber trail in case the evening went sideways and someone discovered his dead body on the beach in the morning. *Ha! Like anyone would be able to figure out who Alejandro is.*

Jack pulled on a new pair of shorts and a cotton tee shirt. Studying himself with a critical eye in the bathroom mirror, he regarded himself as pleasant-looking, six feet tall, decent physique and a flat stomach. Rachel had told him he was above average, whatever the hell that meant—sounded like someone trying to come up with a compliment under duress.

While he brushed his wavy hair in place, a whiff of pipe smoke preceded Alejandro's reflection materializing in the mirror.

"Well, look who's here. I didn't think ghosts had a reflection."

"Ya daft numbskull, 'tis vampires that don't have a reflection." The pirate gave an exasperated sigh.

"Well, pardon me. Don't know many vampires."

"Got any hair gel?" Alejandro removed his hat and fussed with his hair. "Gotta look good for th' ladies tonight."

"Hair gel? How do you even know about hair gel? You're like, over three hundred years old."

The tube of styling gel levitated toward Alejandro. He squirted a small amount in his ghostly hand, and it splattered on the floor. Oblivious, he ran his fingers through his hair, turning from side-to-side admiring his reflection.

"Might be dead, Jack, me boy, but ain't stupid or blind. Been flittin' around this island for centuries. This ol' pirate don't miss much." He adjusted his hat, tucked in his shirt and finger-polished his silver belt buckle.

Jack went into the living room where his laptop sat on the coffee table. Alejandro trailed behind.

"Gotta check my email before we go—do you know what emails are?"

"Avast!" The pirate rolled his eyes. "Have ye not been listenin'?"

He glanced at his inbox and, with a sinking feeling, opened the only new email. It read:

"554 delivery error: Sorry, your message to Rachel@speedymail.com cannot be delivered. This account has been disabled or discontinued."

Jack groaned. Alejandro peered over his shoulder, trying to read the screen. "Whatsa matter, matey?"

"Looks like I just got the closure I wanted. Rachel deactivated her personal email account. I guess I'm 'the one' for tonight. Time to go wenchin'."

"Now yer talkin'. Follow me."

Alejandro floated through the door and headed toward the beach, leaving Jack to lock up.

Jack called out, "Hey, wait up. I can barely see you." He quickly looked around. *Don't want anyone seeing me talking to myself.*

The ghost levitated in place until Jack caught up.

"So, where are we going?"

Alejandro gestured toward the beach bar next door. "Over there, matey."

Jack frowned. "I was just there two nights ago for fish tacos and too many martinis. Can't we go somewhere else?"

"Quit yer whinin', ya pantywaist, and follow me."

He plodded after the gliding ghost. As they drew closer to the bar, strains of music wafted toward them.

Jack's pace quickened, and a smile tugged at his mouth. "Sounds promising."

"Aye! Can feel it in me bones—a good wenchin' night. *Vámonos!*"

A waiter dressed as a pirate greeted Jack as he approached the entrance. "Aaaarrr! Welcome to Pirate Night at the Anchor Bar." Jack hadn't thought about pirates since he was eight years old trying his best to look like Blackbeard. He'd run around the house wearing a skull-and-crossbones hat while brandishing a plastic sword, pretending the family dog was his buccaneer. And now he was surrounded by pirates. One acting, and the other a real, although dead, pirate. *Crazy. No one would ever believe me…*

"Well, shiver me timbers!" Alejandro shimmered in the dim light of the bar. "I'll blend right in."

Jack repeated the phrase in response to the host's greeting. "Well, shiver me timbers."

"Dude, you're pretty quick with the pirate lingo."

"Yeah, you could say I have a good coach."

The man nodded and laughed as if he was in on the joke. "I totally understand, dude. It's half off all drinks tonight, and complimentary appetizers. Our signature cocktail is called Walkin' th' Plank. Give it a try, my friend…if you dare!"

"Sounds dangerous."

"Aaarr!" He rattled the plastic sword at his side. "Three kinds of liquor—all made in the Caribbean. Dark rum, light rum, and spiced rum." He laughed and nodded vigorously. "Never met a pirate who didn't *absolutely love* his rum."

"Good to know."

"Have a seat anywhere you can find room. It's fillin' up fast—Pirate Night's super-duper popular."

"Sure, thanks."

Although covered by a canvas roof, the bar had open sides, and the ocean breeze swept through the place, letting the din of the crowd's chatter escape into the night air. Jack took a few steps onto the sand-covered wooden floor and heard Alejandro mutter, "Mangy cockroach—givin' us pirates a bad name with his lame act."

Jack mumbled, "For once, we agree. Where do you wanna sit?"

"Sit? Belly up to th' bar like a real man. Can't be part of th' action sittin' on yer arse."

Jack rolled his eyes, squeezed into an empty spot at the

packed bar and ordered a beer. Glancing around, he tried to get a fix on Alejandro's whereabouts when he heard a squeal behind him. A waitress, dressed as a pirate's wench, clutched at her backside in response to an unseen force picking up the back of her short, ruffled skirt, exposing her thong bikini and bare ass.

In the muted light, he could make out the ghostly form of Alejandro raising the hem of the waitress's skirt with the tip of his cutlass.

Jack glared at the ghost and quickly positioned himself to block his access to the baffled young woman. "Are you okay?" He raised his brows. "I heard you scream."

"Did you see who did that?" She glanced around, trying to locate the lecher responsible for her embarrassment.

"No, I … I didn't see anything. Sorry."

The waitress stomped off, holding her skirt in place, and disappeared into the kitchen.

Jack grabbed his beer and moved to the other side of the bar, trying to distance himself from the ghost, but Alejandro appeared next to him, laughing.

"What in the hell are you doing? If you're going to cause trouble …"

"Did ya see th' fine poop deck on 'at saucy wench? 'Tis th' most fun this shaggy-arsed pirate's had in over a hundred yar. Like ta bend 'er over th' bar and plunder her pu …"

"Knock it off! Are you out of your mind?" Through pinched lips, Jack said, "If you keep up this bullshit, I'm leaving, and our deal's off …"

"Stop yer carpin', ya lily-livered blowfish, and look o'er there." Alejandro nodded in the direction of a small table in the corner.

Jack stopped his tirade and shifted his gaze. His eyes widened in recognition as the very lovely Jessica Banks captured his attention. She seemed absorbed in her cell phone;

concentration written all over her face. Her long, wavy black hair lay draped over one shoulder. She appeared even prettier than when he'd seen her at his door yesterday morning.

Alejandro's voice shattered his trance. "Don't stare like a one-eyed, lard-brained idiot. Git over there and impress 'er with yer razor-sharp wit. If that don't work, buy 'er that fancy rum drink."

– 6 –

Jack to the Rescue

Jack headed toward Jessica, weaving his way through the crowded, noisy bar. He was surprised how eager he felt to spend time with her, since they'd only had one brief encounter. Apart from her beauty, something else drew him in. *Good energy—positive, upbeat.*

He observed a group of preppy-looking guys decked out in golf shirts and khakis whooping it up near Jessica's table. Two, in particular, had clearly been over-served and sprinkled their conversation with obscenities, the choice words piercing the din. He overheard one lob a lewd comment at their poor waitress, who appeared to be on the verge of tears. Jack frowned. *Assholes on vacation.*

Sensing the pirate on his heels, Jack stopped dead in his tracks. If Alejandro had been a flesh-and-bones person, he would've plowed into him. But, being a ghost, he wound up superimposed on him.

"Get off me! Why in the hell are you tailing me?" Jack shrugged and rolled his shoulders to shake off the sensation of being weighted down.

The pirate took a step back and huffed. "Don't want ye messin' up yer chances with Jessica."

"Oh, please. Like I don't know how to carry on a

conversation with a woman." Jack glanced around. Satisfied no one was watching, he scolded Alejandro through clenched teeth. "The only thing that would mess up my chances is her seeing me talking to a meddling ghost."

"Mighty touchy, ain't ye? Just tryin' to help."

"No need. I don't know why you're so fixated on Jessica, but that's a conversation for another time. For now—*adios*."

Alejandro held up his hands in surrender and disappeared.

As Jack approached Jessica's table, she glanced up and made eye contact with him. She smiled and gave a little wave, setting her cell phone facedown on the table. *Seems happy to see me—so far, so good.*

She gestured at the empty chair next to her. "Hey, Jack. Have a seat."

"Thanks. Enjoying Pirate Night?"

She laughed. "Sure, silly as it is. I like this place. My go-to watering hole, Pirate Night or not." She nodded in the direction of the unruly group. "It's rare that there's a bunch of jerks in here."

"Your go-to place? Must mean you live near here?"

"Yeah—right next door. In fact, we live in the condo directly above yours, on the third floor."

Jack's eyebrows shot up, and he tightened the grip on his bottle of beer, wondering if she'd heard any of the ghost's shenanigans from the night before. *We?* He stole a glance at her left hand, and a knot of dismay formed in his gut. A large opal encircled by diamonds graced her ring finger. He tore his gaze from the impressive gem and yanked himself back to the conversation.

Trying to mask his disappointment, he asked, "You live and work at the same place?"

She nodded. "Yes. Pros and cons to that. The company provides me with a furnished condo… a nice perk."

"Not a bad deal." He cleared his throat, gathering courage. "You mentioned 'we.' You live with somebody?"

"I live with my cat." She chuckled. "He acts more human than feline—you know, attitude all the way."

He smiled, relieved. "A beautiful ring you're wearing. Thought it meant a significant other in your life."

She hesitated. "No. I'm divorced. This ring belonged to my grandma. It's my greatest treasure—probably shouldn't wear it as often as I do, but I can't resist. She was very special to me."

The loud group was making conversation difficult. Jack glanced at her empty glass. "Would you like another drink? I'm ready for a second beer." He pointed to a vacant table. "Want to move over there, away from these obnoxious idiots?"

"Uh, no thanks." She glanced at her cell phone. "I've been here for two drinks and one hour. Time to go—gotta work tomorrow."

His spirits dropped. "Uh, sure. I understand." Forcing a smile, he said, "Nice talking to you, Jessica." *Damn It! Finished before I even started.*

The aroma of pipe smoke wafted by, and he guessed what was coming next. He steeled himself for the ghost's appearance, but thankfully only got a whispered message in his ear. "Offer to walk 'er home, ya addled buffoon."

Jack resisted the impulse to reach out and physically push away the ghost's presence. However, he grabbed at the freshly planted idea and blurted out, "I don't need to stay here either. I'd be happy to walk you home; that is, if you'd like some company."

Jessica smiled and stood. "Sure. Why not?" She removed her sandals when they reached the beach. "Are you enjoying your vacation?"

"Definitely. Sunshine, good rest, jogging on the beach; just what I needed."

"Many people come here to get away from it all. Is that why you're here, Jack?"

Surprised by the question, he hesitated.

"Are you part of a 'we?' Or are you just Jack?" She paused and grinned. "Am I asking too many questions?"

He chuckled. "It's only fair. After all, I asked if you lived with somebody. In fact, I am 'just Jack.' I was engaged until just a few months ago."

"Sometimes breakups are for the best."

"Well, that's putting a positive spin on it. My fiancée decided to wait until our wedding day to call off the engagement."

"Ouch. That's brutal."

Jack nodded. "So yes, this vacation is an escape from reality. Your turn, again. You mentioned you're divorced."

"Yes, a little over a year ago, after a short marriage. Ricky and I grew up together; our parents were best friends. He'd always been a really sweet guy, but I noticed a change in him shortly before we got married. Something wasn't quite right. Well, I ignored my intuition. That, combined with the momentum of wedding plans and our parents' excitement, propelled me toward the altar." She shook her head. "Huge mistake."

Jack nodded, feeling empathetic. "Natural instincts are underrated. Maybe we'd all be better off if we followed our gut. Does your ex still live on the island?"

"Thankfully, no. The last I knew he enrolled in Miami Dade's electrician program."

"I imagine you would've run into him quite a bit on an island this small."

"Yes. He had a hard time accepting the divorce, so I'm glad he's gone."

Jack noticed the lights of the condominium complex twinkling ahead in the darkness and wished the beach walk could last longer. He wanted to savor the balmy Caribbean evening and Jessica's company.

A voice from behind cut into their conversation. "How 'bout sharin' that Caribbean Princess? Not fair you got her all to yourself."

Jack spun around and recognized one of the jerks from the bar, wearing a cocky grin and holding a drink. The man lunged at Jessica in an attempt to grab her arm. She dodged his advance, and Jack maneuvered himself to stand directly in front of the drunken idiot, protecting her.

The man raised his drink in the air and shouted over Jack's shoulder, "Hey, Island Girl, I can show you a better time than this douchebag." He grabbed his crotch, as if that was all the convincing she'd need.

Jack raised his voice. "Get outta here. Go back to the bar."

"Ooh, tough guy. Whatcha gonna do—kick my ass?" He tried to reach around Jack and grope Jessica, but Jack blocked his move. "C'mon, all I want is a sample of that dee-licious poontang."

Acting on instinct, Jack shifted his weight, pushed off with his right foot and launched a solid punch into the drunk's nose.

The guy howled, and his drink went flying. Clutching his face, he fell like a sack of flour to the sand, blood seeping through his fingers. He bellowed, "You broke my fuckin' nose, man!"

Lurching toward him, just a few yards away, Jack recognized his obnoxious friend. *Oh shit, not another one.* He shook his throbbing hand, not eager to throw another punch.

A movement in Jack's peripheral vision caught his attention. Alejandro appeared in a puff of wind and, with lightning speed, tripped the advancing man, landing him flat on his back gasping for air. He drew his cutlass and held the curved blade at the man's throat.

"Ya mangy cockroach!"

Uncertain what kind of damage Alejandro could inflict with his ghostly weapon, Jack yelled, "Alejandro! Stop!"

The ghost shot a look at Jack and tucked the cutlass back under his belt.

The downed man found his breath and attempted to get up. Alejandro gave a mirthless laugh and kicked him in the ribs, knocking him back to the sand. "Go ahead—try an' get up an' run, ya flea-bitten coward—me loves a movin' target."

As the man struggled to his knees, Jessica ran toward him holding a small canister. She sprayed the contents into his eyes. He screamed and grabbed at his face, scrambling to scurry away, the soft beach offering little traction. Showing no concern for his groaning, broken-nosed friend, he ran back toward the bar, stumbling and kicking up sand the entire way.

Jack rushed to Jessica's side. "Are you okay?" He glanced around. No more drunks. No more ghost. Everything had happened so fast. *Did she see Alejandro?*

"I guess so." She looked up at him with a shaky smile and put her hand on his arm. "Better than him." She pointed to the man holding his broken nose and trying to get into a standing position, but failing. He ended up on his knees, throwing up in the sand. "Let's get out of here before this halfwit can cause any more trouble."

"Should we call the police?"

"Can't think of one good reason to do that, Jack. It's over. You handled a drunk, and that's it."

"All right. We're outta here."

They hurried down the beach and reached the condo resort in a couple of minutes.

Jessica gestured toward the pool. "There's a bench, let's sit for a minute." She drew a deep breath. "I've never been in a situation like that before. I've run into the occasional jerk, but never someone threatening. I don't know what I would've done if you hadn't been there."

"Oh, you would've sprayed him to death." Jack put his arm around her and gave a little squeeze. "The thought of that jackass laying a hand on you was too much."

"You're a real gentleman—Gentleman Jack. Has a nice ring to it. Anyone ever call you that before?"

"Nope. You're the first."

She glanced down, and her eyes widened. "Oh no! Your hand's bloody. I've got first aid supplies in my condo."

Seize the opportunity or play the tough guy? "I'm okay. Nothing serious, I'm sure."

"How can you be sure? It's dark out here. C'mon. I won't take no for an answer."

"Okay, but promise you'll be gentle with me."

– 7 –

First Aid and Flirting

Jack and Jessica approached their building, and Jessica led the way to the third floor. Despite the beach drama and his bloodied hand, Jack tuned into the view of her shapely little rear end as she climbed up the stairs.

She fished the keys from her purse and opened the door. "All my supplies are in the bathroom—just around the corner."

Jack followed her inside, noting the chic, tropical decorating style. Colorful floral print cushions covered rattan furniture. The ceiling fan, with wooden blades resembling palm fronds, kicked up a subtle breeze. The walls, painted in soothing pastels, complemented the white marble floors. A glass-topped dining room table tinted blue looked like the calm surface of the ocean. His apartment was bachelor-boring by comparison. Content with the basics, he'd spent no time making his place look homey or inviting.

Jessica squirted soap in the bathroom sink and ran the water until a suitable amount of suds appeared. "There—put your hands in and wash off that blood."

He plunged his hands into the water and smiled. *Such a little mother hen. Like I don't know how to wash my hands.*

"Is that water temperature okay?" She frowned and tested the water.

He squeezed her soapy fingers. "You're sweet. Thanks for taking care of me."

She tossed him a mischievous look. "Hope I'm gentle enough for you." Pulling his hand from the water, she studied the damage. "I think the blood was the other guy's. Don't see any abrasions—although a couple of your knuckles are swollen." She trailed one finger across the reddened spot and glanced at him. "My professional opinion? You'll likely live through this."

He grinned, enjoying her playful manner.

Jessica pulled a clean towel from a wicker basket and wrapped up his hand. "There you go! Almost as good as new."

"How 'bout you? You doing okay?"

She closed her eyes and sighed. "I am now, but I was scared earlier."

He enjoyed a sense of gratification—he'd protected her from a threatening situation. *With some ghostly help*. "Nothing to worry about. Those cowards are long gone. I guarantee it."

A spark flickered in her eyes. "Who's Alejandro?"

"Alejandro?" He tried to keep a neutral expression on his face.

"Yes. You called out that name on the beach, and then you said to 'stop.' Stop what?"

"I, um, I don't remember saying that. Maybe you heard wrong?"

She shrugged. "Maybe. After all, it was in the heat of the moment. Hey, how 'bout that second beer? You've certainly earned it."

"Don't you have to get up early for work tomorrow?"

She checked her watch. "It's only 11:00—it's not like I have a long commute."

"Sure. A beer would be great." *Why not?* He was enjoying himself with a woman—something he hadn't experienced in a while.

She smiled and headed for the kitchen. Pulling a couple

of bottles from the refrigerator, she gestured to the bar stools surrounding the kitchen island. "Have a seat," she said, popping the tops and handing him a chilled brew.

He sat and took a long pull, grateful for the overhanging counter, which hid the effect she had on him. He felt embarrassed. *Just like a hormonal teenager.*

The aroma of pipe smoke wafted under Jack's nose, accompanied by Alejandro's unwelcome voice invading his ear. "Kinda early to be raisin' yer Jolly Roger."

Jack squeezed his eyes shut, trying to block out the bawdy pirate.

"Is everything okay?"

He snapped to attention. "Sure. Why?"

"You had a strange look on your face. Does the beer taste all right? It's a local brew called Ironshore Ale. It isn't for everyone; maybe you'd like something else?"

"Oh, the beer's tasty." His face heated up. "Uh, just a sidetracked thought." He forged on. "Have you always lived on this island?"

"Mostly. When I was eighteen, I left and went to the US for my college education. Lived there for six years."

"Where'd you go to school?"

"Michigan State University—the School of Hospitality Business."

He grinned. "I went there too—the business college."

"Cool! Fellow Sparties," said Jessica, and raised her beer bottle. "We must've been there around the same time."

"Two thousand six through thirteen?"

She nodded. "Two thousand nine through fifteen. What was your favorite bar?"

"Hands down, Crunchy's."

"We must've crossed paths at that place. I logged in some hours there. Loved their bucket specials."

"Yeah. What was it ... with every bucket of beer, you had to order two buckets of greasy bar food, right?"

"Yup. How 'bout The Riv? Best tater tots in town for two bucks."

"Yeah, great spot. Good memories. How'd you like MSU? And the Great Lakes state? A huge school, and a totally different climate for you."

"I had a lot of good times at MSU. Loved the school, but the weather…" She rolled her eyes.

"I'm sure that took some getting used to, coming from a place with perpetual summer."

"It did, but I came to enjoy the change of seasons. Here it's basically the same weather, with a temperature swing from seventy to ninety degrees."

"Were you tempted to stay in the States?"

"Yes and no. My family's here, plus I had what I thought was a dream job waiting for me, managing a small boutique hotel. And then there was Ricky." She smirked. "Maybe I should've stayed in the States."

Jessica gestured in Jack's direction. "So, you came to Grand Cayman to thaw out from Michigan's winter?"

"Yup. Good to be here."

Simultaneously, she said, "Good to have you here."

They laughed and clinked their bottles together.

"How'd you pick Grand Cayman?" asked Jessica.

"Cayman picked me. I'm here for business and vacation. I inherited an account, Caribbean Marine, from one of our sales reps that retired. I meet with them tomorrow morning for the first time. I also have a customer located in Miami. This island's just a short plane ride away from there, so it's a good fit."

"Nice. So, what's your job?"

"Yacht sales rep. I sell mid-sized yachts for Noble Yachts, a Michigan-based company—the boats have been manufactured there for about the last fifty years."

"How cool is that? What a great job. I love boats."

"You'd really love these… beautiful, luxurious."

"Do you own one?"

"No. But I get to take them out on the water with my customers."

"So, you get a taste of the good life, huh?"

"Yes... on someone else's dime."

"How'd you find out about the Sandy Beach Resort? As property manager, I'm curious."

Jack gave a half-smile. "Actually, the owner of the company I work for, Johnathan Noble, set up this vacation for me as a kind of reward. Plus a break from, you know, the whole aborted marriage thing."

"What a super guy." Jessica lifted an eyebrow. "You must love your job."

Jack chuckled. "Love is a little strong. Let's say I really like it. How 'bout you? Do you love your job?"

"Not really. I'd like to own my own inn or B & B someday. But this job pays well. Can't complain."

Jack turned and glanced out the window, noticing the ghostly silhouette of Alejandro.

"Jessica..."

"Yes?"

"Kind of a bizarre question, but since you've lived here most of your life, well, have you ever seen any ghosts?"

Her eyes grew wide, and she burst out laughing. "You're telling me you've seen a duppy?"

"Wh-what's a duppy?"

"It's Caribbean patois for ghost or spirit."

"What's patois?"

"Ah, Jack, you've much to learn about the islands. Caribbean patois is a local dialect usually associated with Jamaica, but spoken throughout the Caribbean."

"Can you speak patois?"

She put her hands on her hips and said, "Yuh nuh think yuh too ole fi believe inna duppy?"

He laughed. "Translation, please?"

"Don't you think you're too old to believe in ghosts?"

"I don't know—what's age have to do with it?"

"My grandma used to blame everything on the duppies. She'd misplace or lose something and say, 'It's them damn duppies, movin' my stuff around.'"

"Did *you* ever see a ghost?"

"No. But many have." She sipped her beer. "There's a place out in the wop-wops that was haunted by a pirate ghost several years ago. It'd been an old private estate, later converted into an inn. The owner declared bankruptcy and they shuttered the place. Since then, no stories."

"Interesting." His grip tightened on the beer bottle. *Pirate ghost?* "Um, what's a wop-wop?"

She chuckled. "It's like the middle of nowhere, you know, out in the sticks."

"Duppies, patois, and wop-wops. I'm getting an education on island culture tonight."

Jessica leaned in and tapped her finger on Jack's hand. "So, have you seen a ghost?"

"Maybe."

She nodded. "Okay. Where?"

"Downstairs. In the condo I'm renting."

"Were you scared?"

He grinned and shook his head. "I ain't afraid of no ghosts."

"Ah, *Ghostbusters*; loved that movie. Let me know if you see your duppy again. As the property manager, I should know about," she waggled her eyebrows and whispered, "spooky things."

"You're delightful, Jessica. I'll keep you posted on my ghost." He unwrapped his hand and placed the towel on the counter. "Time for me to go."

They strolled to the door. Jessica lifted her chin, making eye contact. "I enjoy being with you. You're a nice guy—thanks again for coming to my rescue."

"Thanks for the beer *and* the first aid. Will I see you around tomorrow?"

"Probably. I'm almost always on the property."

Shake her hand? A goodnight hug? He felt something brush against his leg, interrupting his internal debate. He stepped back, narrowly missing a large orange tabby cat.

"Oh, Carrots, there you are." Jessica scooped up the purring cat. "He came out to greet you—a rare event. That puts you in the category of 'special guest.'"

Carrots turned his head and stared at Jack as if evaluating him. He tentatively extended a paw in Jack's direction.

"Maybe he wants to shake hands." He took the offered paw and shook it.

"That's a first," said Jessica. "I think he's smitten with you."

The cat, abruptly done with pleasantries, struggled to be released and jumped from Jessica's arms.

Jack took her hand. "You know, animals are very intuitive..."

She stood on her tiptoes and kissed him on the cheek. "Goodnight, Jack."

An angry meow shattered the peace, and Jessica stepped away from Jack. He shook his head at the cat, who sat like a sentinel at the doorway to what he assumed was the bedroom. "Your four-legged protector. I wonder how he'd fare with drunks on the beach?"

Ricky Wills peered through the powerful 30x80 trail binoculars and focused on Jessica's kitchen window. Hidden by darkness and a sizable bougainvillea bush, he was free to observe, just like he'd watched the dramatic altercation on the beach.

About an hour ago he'd been aimlessly walking the beach,

waiting. He had watched Jessica head for the bar next door, and decided to hang around. It was mostly dark when he picked out the familiar shape of his wife, or more accurately his ex-wife, in the distance, and she wasn't alone. Ricky could tell she was with a man, which pissed him off, and imagined how fun it'd be to surprise the two of them. *Hey, Jessie. Glad to see me? Who's this jerk?*

He walked toward them, eager for a confrontation, but another man, clearly drunk, came up behind them, followed closely by his equally wasted friend. Ricky held back and watched as the drama and fight unfolded. He couldn't believe his bad luck. The strangers had stolen his fun, not to mention the element of surprise. Jessica, along with her mystery man, hurried away, leaving the first assailant puking in the sand. His curiosity on overdrive, Ricky had followed Jessica and the man back to her condo.

Now, fury pumped through his veins as he viewed Jessica saying her flirty goodnight to the pretty-boy hero she'd picked up at the bar. Even the cat made a guest appearance. *How cozy.* No need for audio, as her body language said it all. *The little slut's enjoying herself.*

When the man left, Ricky watched him walk down to the second floor. *How convenient.* He grunted. *Low-life renter. He'll be around a week or two, then off to his real life. Plenty of time to dabble in the island goody bag, though.* He cracked his neck, side-to-side, and then huffed a deep breath. *Whoever this asshole is, he is won't get very far.*

A whiff of pipe smoke interrupted his choleric thoughts. Ricky glanced around, but saw nothing out of the ordinary. *Probably some old fuck smoking on his balcony.* He refocused and trained the field glasses back on Jessica. Looking all happy-happy, she stood at the kitchen sink and removed her ring before washing her hands. He smirked. *I'd wash too if I handled that filthy cat.*

No fan of Carrots, he'd experienced the business end of his claws the last time he was in Jessica's condo. Uninvited, Ricky had let himself in with a master key to snoop around her bedroom, looking for signs of a man in her life. The only thing he found was Carrots asleep at the end of the bed. As if the cat understood he was up to no good, he'd pounced on Ricky, leaving bloody scratch marks on his arm.

When the light went out in the window, a light switched on in Ricky's brain. A giddy, Christmas-like feeling washed over him. He let the binoculars drop to his side. A present in the form of an opportunity had just landed in his lap. *The opal ring, of course. Her prized possession.* He touched the master key in his pocket. His chest expanded with a sense of superiority. Was he just that smart, or was it his razor-sharp instincts? Didn't matter. He was always prepared, just like a Boy Scout.

Fully expecting Alejandro to appear the moment he stepped outside Jessica's condo, Jack felt surprised to be alone—and that he even kind of missed the pirate. He wouldn't mind debriefing the evening with someone, even a ghostly someone.

He set the alarm on his cell phone and then got into bed. Scenes from the night replayed in his head, and he wondered about the possible consequences for punching the drunk on the beach. For sure, he wouldn't be returning to the Anchor Bar for the rest of his stay. No need to risk running into that fool again.

Far more pleasant thoughts of Jessica nudged out the memories of the fight, and Jack rehashed every comment and gesture. She'd called him a nice guy, and what the hell did that mean? *Kind of a vanilla description, even a bit cliché.* He admonished himself. *Stop overthinking it.*

Just before drifting off to sleep, he wondered if Alejandro had crossed over. *I kept my promise. One night out. Period.*

– 8 –

A New Problem for Jack

The cell phone alarm pierced Jack's sleep bubble with the sound of electronic songbirds. He stretched and rolled over to grab his phone. Although his morning vision was blurry, there was no mistaking Jessica's opal and diamond ring sitting on the bedside stand.

He shot up in bed, grabbed the ring and stared. "Wha . . . ?" He shook his head, trying to clear the sleep from his brain. "How the fuck did this get here?" Anger swept over him, and he raised his voice in case the ghost was within earshot. "Goddammit, Alejandro! I know you're behind this." The chirping birds yammered on. He rubbed his eyes and winced as he fumbled the phone into silence. His right hand smarted, puffy and red with the early stages of bruising. *A ghost, a fight, a stolen ring, and I've only been here three days.*

He sighed as he palmed the ring and stared at it, willing it to go away. Now he was forced to muster patience and wait until dark to confront the thieving pirate, whom he hadn't even wanted to see again. He checked the weather app—*sunset at 6:15*. The current time showed 7:00 AM. The ghost had never appeared in daylight, so Jack figured he was in for about a twelve-hour wait; that is, if Alejandro was still around.

Jack threw on a tee shirt and shorts and mucked about

in the kitchen making coffee, contemplating his situation. Making a good first impression at Caribbean Marine had to be today's top priority, so he forced himself to put the ring problem on hold. After all, the ring couldn't come to any harm if it was in his possession. Equipped with a coffee carafe, bowl of cereal and his laptop, he padded to the screened-in porch, sat and reviewed his notes for the upcoming meeting. He then organized the promotional materials he'd brought with him, catalogs and brochures, and put them in presentation folders embossed with the Noble Yacht logo. Judging from the lackluster sales his predecessor posted, he realized he had some work to do.

Jack glanced at the time and headed for the shower. He selected the highest pressure setting on the shower head, allowing Jessica's opal ring to creep into his thoughts again as the water pounded down. He vigorously shampooed his head hoping it'd stimulate his brain, and an answer to his problem would materialize. *What the hell am I going to do?* His imagination conjured up a hypothetical scene. *"Hey, Jessica—here's your ring. You'll never believe this, but that ghost I mentioned last night? Well, he stole your ring and put it on my bedside stand. Found it there this morning—isn't that the craziest thing? What? You don't believe me? You think I'm a thieving liar?"*

A niggling voice told him that honesty was always the best policy, but he argued that away. *The truth's too bizarre. She'll never believe a ghost could or would pull a prank like that.*

After his shower and shave, Jack put on cotton khaki trousers, a crisp white shirt, no tie, and a navy blue linen blazer. Most likely anybody he'd see today would be dressed far more casually, but he believed a sales rep's clothes should be a cut above. After all, he was the one asking for orders.

At the last minute, he tucked the opal ring among his folded clothing in the dresser drawer. *Don't need anyone from housekeeping seeing that.*

He packed his leather brief bag. *Wonder if I'll see Jessica today?* Part of him wanted to, part of him was wary. He pictured her upset about the missing ring, and then what would he do? He fought back the stress that threatened to drive him to distraction.

Jack left the condo, headed for the parking lot and a taxi to take him to Caribbean Marine. He took a deep breath, absorbing the sunny tropical day.

"Good morning, Jack."

His heart lurched at the now-familiar voice, and he momentarily froze. *The ring. I should tell her about the ring.* He spun around and faced Jessica, his anxiety tempered by his delight at seeing her. She wore a cornflower blue crocheted skirt and a sleeveless white blouse that accentuated her toned, brown arms.

"Hey, good morning, Jessica. How ya doing? Any symptoms of post-traumatic stress from last night's adventure?"

"I'm doing well, thanks to you. Bet we can't say the same for the guy with the broken nose."

Jack grimaced. "Yeah—I'm trying not to think about that. I've never hit anyone that hard before." He flexed his sore hand from the memory.

Jessica laid her hand on his arm. "Well, he had it coming. Drunk and dangerous—a wicked combo."

She smiled. "You look nice. Very professional."

"Thanks."

Jessica shaded her eyes from the sun and met Jack's eye. "Um … no guests are checking in this afternoon, so I, uh, have a couple of free hours and wondered if you'd like to have lunch? That is, if you're done with the business part of your day by then."

Surprised, he paused, realizing she was asking him out.

"I'd love to have lunch with you."

She wrinkled her nose. "Are you sure? You hesitated."

"Me? No. No hesitation here." He ran his fingers through his hair. "I'm just surprised—but pleasantly so, of course—you know, you're busy working here... so what time and where?"

"Meet me at the administration office at one o'clock." Her impish grin told him she delighted in flustering him. "There's a fun beach joint, called The Wreck Bar at Rum Point, on the north side of the island. I'll drive."

"Great. Well—looking forward to it."

"We've got lots to discuss. Good luck today. See you later." She fluttered her fingers in a little wave and turned around.

Jack returned the wave. *What does she mean by "lots to discuss?" Does she think I had something to do with her missing ring? Does she even know her ring's missing? These stupid ghost pranks are going to kill me.*

– 9 –

Lunch and Romance

"Hi, Jessica." Jack got into her Prius. "You been waiting long?"

"No. Thought I'd cool the car for you. You Snowbelt people take a while to acclimate to our hot weather."

"That's true. Couldn't wait to swap my long pants for short ones."

"I'll bet. How was Caribbean Marine today?" Jessica put the car in gear and zipped out into the road, merging with the heavy traffic.

"Great. I was there for a couple of hours."

"That's a good sign, yes?"

He nodded. "They showed me around before our meeting. That place sells everything from fishing gear to kayaks to yachts."

"I've driven by their store but never walked in. It's a nice building. Did they buy anything from you?"

"The owner really likes our sportier models. They have wide appeal—good for cruising or fishing. Open bow, outboard engines. They range from thirty-four to thirty-eight feet. I'm working on him to buy one for his showroom floor."

"Think he'll do it?"

"A good chance. I'm going to follow up with him before I leave. The previous sales rep from our company, an older guy that retired, only came here a couple of times. You gotta show up more often to cultivate a relationship and, of course, to sell more boats."

"Does that mean you'll be coming back here?" Jessica smiled.

"I hope so." He returned her smile. "I kinda like this little island."

Jessica wheeled into an unpaved parking lot, gravel crunching under the tires of the Prius. "Welcome to Rum Point, the best beach on the north side of the island, and home of the Mudslide."

"Mudslide?"

"You'll see. Come on."

They walked onto the beach, and Jessica pointed to a table just outside the entrance to a tiny, lime-green clapboard-sided bar. "Let's sit here. We can dig our feet into the sand while we have lunch."

"Sure. Looks great." Jack gestured at a lone pelican resting on an old wooden piling by the surf, who seemed undisturbed by a small catamaran gliding in for a beach landing. "Did you queue up this postcard scene just for me?"

"Yeah. A Chamber of Commerce moment. Natural beauty is the island's bread and butter. We Caymanians joke we're in the business of selling sunshine to snowbirds."

"Summertime in February. Feels like heaven to this snowbird." His gaze strayed to a young woman who looked remarkably like Halle Barry. He turned toward Jessica and whispered, "She looks just like the actress…"

Jessica followed his glance and chuckled. "Yes, she does. That's my friend, Sarah. She'd be flattered by your comment."

She waved and called out, "Hi Sarah." She pointed to Jack. "He'll have a Mudslide, and I'll have a Diet Coke."

"What? No Mudslide for you? *And* you're ordering for me on our first date?"

"I'm a take-charge kind of girl. Besides, you must try a

Mudslide. It's a touristy thing, but delicious. You'll love it. I have to work this afternoon, so no drinks for me."

He smiled, relieved by her playfulness, suggesting she wasn't stressed or worried. *Must mean she doesn't know her ring's missing.*

"Take charge anytime, I'm putty in your hands." Inwardly he grimaced. *Geez. Flirting with old, cheesy lines.*

Sarah approached with the drinks on a tray. "You must be Jack. I understand you're a Mudslide virgin. Here ya go." She plunked a frothy, chocolaty, creamy-looking concoction in front of him. A red and white striped paper straw poked up through the decadence.

"You girls were talking about me behind my back?" He shot a glance in Jessica's direction.

"Not talking—just texting."

He felt himself blush, flattered to be the subject of female interest. "This drink looks like dessert."

"Looks like dessert, tastes like dessert—hits ya like a pirate ship. Go ahead—take a sip through the straw."

He inwardly smirked at the pirate ship comment and took a long pull on the straw. A blast of chilled liquor slid down his throat. "Wow! What's in this drink?"

The two women laughed. "The first swallow is all Kahlua," Jessica explained, "followed by a combo of Bailey's Irish Cream, vodka, and chocolate sauce."

"The bartender squirts Kahlua down the straw," said Sarah. "Catches you by surprise. You like?"

"I'm sold—my new favorite drink."

She grinned at Jessica and said, "I'll be back to take your lunch order."

Jessica sipped on her soft drink and stared at Jack. "I did some research this morning."

He raised his eyebrows. "Research?"

"Uh-huh."

"What kind of research?"

"The ghostly kind."

"What do you mean?" He furrowed his brow, feigning confusion.

"Last night, I told you about an inn that was haunted by a pirate ghost." She idly stirred her Coke with a straw.

"The one that closed due to bankruptcy?"

"That's right. I couldn't remember the details of the story, so I asked my mom about it."

"And?"

"She told me the ghost's name was Alejandro."

Jack's eyes widened. "Okay. So what's that got to do with anything?"

Jessica shook her finger at him in a teasing manner, a smile tugging at her mouth. "Oh, please. Don't play dumb with me. You called out the name 'Alejandro' on the beach last night, and when I asked you about it, you acted cagey. Later, you asked me if I'd ever seen any ghosts on the island. Coincidental, wouldn't you say?"

Time to come clean. He closed his eyes for a moment, sorting his thoughts, then ran his fingers through his hair and fixed his gaze on Jessica.

"Okay. Here's what happened. My first night here, this misty-looking shape appeared in my bedroom. In the morning, I wondered if it'd all been a dream. But it came back the next night and turned out to be a ghost—a pirate ghost, no less. He introduced himself as Alejandro, 'the greatest pirate to ever sail the Caribbean.'" Jack paused. "Do you think I'm crazy?"

"Absolutely not. I'm on pins and needles, just taking it all in." She reached over, laid her hand on top of his. "Please, go on."

Encouraged, he continued and told her of his encounter with the ghostly pirate, leading up to the night at the bar. Somewhere during the story, another Mudslide showed up.

He finished his story with Alejandro appearing on the beach from thin air, handling the drunk with ease.

Jessica's expression was rapt; eyes wide and focused. "Unbelievable. This ghost seems to have attached himself to you in a big way."

"I guess so. I've only one-and-a-half days of vacation left, and he's supposed to cross over—permanently—to the other side by the time I leave. Oh, and he seems to have a particular interest in you. Even mentioned you by name. Know anything about that?"

"No, I don't. I've never seen this ghost." She shook her head, a mystified look on her face. "How crazy is it that a ghost can actually speak, and then asks about me by name?"

"I know. If someone told me the same story, I'd be super skeptical." He hesitated. "I'm grateful you believe me. I'd rather share the Alejandro experience than go it alone."

Jessica nodded. "My mother told me she experienced some ghostly intervention when she was newly married. She had boiled some water in a large saucepan. The pot's handle hung over the stove's edge. She accidentally bumped the handle, and knocked it off the burner." Jessica paused and smiled. "Mom said it was like a cartoon scene. The saucepan stopped falling in mid-air and the spilling water poured itself back into the pot. The whole thing ended up back on the stove."

"Wow. That's a close call," said Jack. "Sounds kinda ghostly to me."

"She thought so too. Whoever—or whatever—it was prevented her from sustaining serious burns."

"Seems like a friendly ghost. Maybe a protector. Wonder if this Alejandro ghost was involved in that incident?"

"Who knows? I'm glad you told me about him. After all, duppies or ghosts are part of our culture."

"I don't need to see him again," said Jack. "I agreed to spend *only* one night with him in the bar, which was last night.

However, this ghost doesn't seem the type to hold up his end of deals made and agreed upon."

"What time does he usually show up?" She asked the question like an idea had grabbed her.

"Um, after dark. Why?"

"I'd love to see him!"

"You would?"

"Sure. Among the locals, he's a legend. And if he has to cross over soon—could be my only opportunity."

Jack took Jessica's hand and kissed it. "Looks like you just garnered yourself an invitation to dinner tonight—at my place. Eight o'clock. Don't be late."

"Can't refuse an invitation like that. I'll be there. Now, how would you like some lunch to go with those Mudslides?"

Slouched in the passenger seat and slightly buzzed, the combination of drinks, lunch, sun, and a beautiful woman put a romantic twist on the afternoon. Jack's senses perked up as the first soft chords of Jason Mraz's acoustic guitar playing "I Won't Give Up" came through the radio. He sang along to the sentimental lyrics.

"Hey, you have a nice voice," said Jessica.

"I was in the High School Glee Club. Women went crazy over my voice."

"Is that right? You're not exaggerating, are you?"

"Maybe." He winked, squeezed her hand, glanced out the window and pointed to a lonely stretch of beach. "Do you mind pulling over?"

"Sure. Are you okay?"

"More than okay."

Jessica parked the car under a palm tree and turned toward

Jack, her deep brown eyes soft and expressive. "What's on your mind, Jack?"

"You. You're on my mind."

"Go on." She tipped her head and smiled, holding his gaze.

"A quiet beach, nobody's around—would you like to hang out for a while—if you have time?"

She touched his arm. "Love to. I don't think anyone at the office will care if I'm away a bit longer. There's a beach blanket on the seat behind you. Standard gear when you live on a Caribbean island."

Ricky wheeled into a parking spot at the Tiki-Hut restaurant directly across the street from the narrow strip of beach. He grabbed his binoculars, picked the table closest to the road for optimum viewing, and then ordered two shots of tequila and a beer.

He focused on Jessica's car, which was parked just off the road on the shoulder. His skin prickled with irritation when he noticed someone was with her. In an attempt to stay calm, he congratulated himself on his latest brilliant act. The "RealTyme" GPS tracker he'd stuck underneath Jessica's car allowed him to monitor her every movement. Hell, the thing alerted him by text and email anytime her car budged, *plus* he could view her route on a Google map. *Well worth the sixty-nine dollars.*

When his cell phone chirped, notifying him of her car moving, he was working at his job with Crystal Clear Pools and unable to act. But the stalking gods were on his side. Since she'd been gone quite a while, all the way up to Rum Point he noted, he was able to catch up with her returning to Seven Mile Beach.

He made a slight adjustment to the binoculars' focus and felt enraged to see that same guy from the night before with her. *You jerk-off. I'll bet you still have that ring and are too chicken-shit to tell her.*

Ricky had been so pleased with his clever idea of stealing Jessica's opal ring and relocating it to the guy's condo. He still had a master key to the condos from when he'd worked there, shortly after he and Jessica split. Not a patient man, he expected immediate results. He assumed Jessica would blame the guy for lifting her ring and then throw him out of the condo, just like she threw him out over a year ago. But that didn't happen. The jerk was still in the picture, vacationing his ass off.

Jack grabbed the blanket and waited as Jessica took off her sandals. He admired the slight arch of her feet, manicured toes polished with a cotton candy pink. His gaze traveled up her ankles and shapely leg. She caught him checking her out, and gave him a sly smile.

They got out of the car and strolled through the sand. "How about this shady spot?" asked Jack, gesturing to a nearby palm tree.

They spread out the tropical print coverlet on the sand and settled in, side-by-side. The ocean breeze ruffled Jessica's hair. Jack reached out and tucked a wayward lock behind her ear. His hand trailed down to her waist, and he pulled her close, her head resting on his shoulder.

"You're amazing, Jessica," murmured Jack, speaking just above the low rumble of the waves.

She glanced up at him and smiled. "You're in vacation mode."

He furrowed his brow. "What's that mean?"

"Many people come and go every day on this romantic little island." She toyed with a white shell shaped like a baby's ear.

"Are you suggesting I'm reacting to this place and not you?" He straightened, hearing the serious tone in her comment.

"Maybe. I don't want to end up on the wrong side of a vacation romance."

"Do you think I'm a vacation fling kind of a guy?"

She shrugged. "I'm not saying that. But emotionally you're in kind of a strange place, aren't you?"

"You mean my aborted wedding?"

"Yes. I'll confess, the word 'rebound' is flashing like a neon sign in my head."

"I didn't come to Cayman to have a one or two-night stand, Jessica. I'm just not wired that way."

"Did you ever figure out why your fiancée deserted you on your wedding day?"

"No." Jack took a deep breath and let it out slowly. "It'd be nice to have some closure on the whole mess. But I don't think that's going to happen. Rachel hasn't talked, texted, or written to me since that day."

"How long ago was it?"

"About three-and-a-half months—mid-October."

"How are you doing now?"

"Right now, I'm happy being here with you."

"Do you still love her?"

"No, I don't." Jack hesitated while questions of his own found a voice. "What about you and your ex?"

She puffed out a breath. "I haven't loved Ricky for a long time." She turned to face Jack and put her hand on his chest. "Let's leave them in the past. They didn't deserve us anyway."

He closed his eyes and sought her lips, barely brushing them with his. With that whispery touch his world fell away, along with the past. She shivered, and then leaned into him, deepening their kiss. The dappled sunlight, the sound of the ocean, and Jessica's responsive mouth breathed life into him, awakening an intense desire he hadn't felt in a long time. They fell back on the blanket, their bodies pressed together.

The squeals of children fast approaching had the effect of a needle scraping across a vinyl record. The sound of a beach ball bouncing on the sand interrupted their kiss, just before the ball landed on top of Jessica.

They scrambled to a sitting position. Jessica said, "What the hell? Where did these kids come from?"

Jack shook his head, trying to switch gears from passion to practicality.

Three little boys came flying at them like a pack of puppies. The tallest kid hit the sand as if he was stealing a base, plowing to a stop in front of Jack. "Hey, mister! Did my beach ball hit you guys?"

"It did. You should watch what you're doing." Jack scowled as he got to his feet.

The three boys screamed and jumped, high-fiving each other. The same kid spoke again. "The man said he'd give us five dollars each if we hit you guys with the beach ball."

Jack frowned. "What man?"

"The man across the street."

Jack turned, looking for the mysterious instigator.

"Do you know this man?" asked Jessica.

"No."

"Where are your parents?"

"Having lunch at that restaurant." The kid pointed to the Tiki-Hut restaurant across the street. He crossed his arms and frowned, taking a defensive stance. "They said we could play on the beach."

"I don't see anybody standing across the street." Jack faced the boys. "Can you point out the man who talked to you?"

They turned toward the street and squinted. "He's gone." The gleeful expressions on the three turned to dismay as they realized no man, no cash.

"Come on, guys! Let's see if we can find him." The boys took off at a dead run, leaving their beach ball behind.

Jack raised his eyebrows. "Good luck with that. If this weren't so weird and creepy, it'd be funny." He held his hand out to Jessica, helping her to stand, and then drew her into a hug.

She sighed. "I was just thinking the same thing. Who would do that?"

He leaned back, making eye contact. "I don't know. But, I do know that you're very special, Jessica."

She smiled. "I've enjoyed being with you, Jack, and I'd like nothing more than to stay here all afternoon, but I should get back to work."

"All right. I need time to prepare dinner for my hot date, anyways."

Jessica kissed him on the cheek and whispered, "She's a lucky girl."

Ricky refocused his binoculars, sharpening the scene of Jessica and her new boy-toy spreading out the beach blanket. *How fucking cozy.* When they kissed, he fought the urge to hurl his chair against the Tiki-Hut's wall. He muttered through clenched teeth, "Keep your mother-fuckin' hands off my wife!"

The sound of kids kicking around a beach ball in the restaurant's parking lot penetrated his rage. He recognized an opportunity, raced out to the three boys, and made his business proposal. The kids took the bait and moved their play across the street to the beach.

Delighted with his quick thinking, he hurried back to his table and trained the binoculars on the beach scene. When the beach ball hit Jessica, he fist-pumped. *Take that, bitch.*

His mood brightened—he'd successfully manipulated the little rug-rats into interrupting Jessica's make-out session. Having no intention of paying the five dollars each he'd promised them, he threw back the rest of his beer and snuck out the side door without paying his tab. *Mission accomplished.*

– 10 –

Champagne and a Surprise

As luck would have it, Ricky drove by the condos just as Jessica's mystery man climbed into a cab at the curb. Puffed up from his recent success at the Tiki-Hut, and buzzing from the beer and tequila, he regarded this chance encounter as confirmation that yes, he was on the right track to reclaiming Jessica. Otherwise, why would he have been gifted this new opportunity from the stalking gods?

Ricky followed the cab through a few miles of congested traffic, until it finally turned into the parking lot of the upscale grocery store, Kirk Market. Jessica's boyfriend got out, grabbed a cart and entered the store. Ricky parked his car and did the same, delighted he could openly follow the guy around and observe his every move.

Trying to appear like a normal shopper, Ricky randomly tossed grocery items in his cart as he made his way up and down the aisles. He watched the man select lobster tails and shrimp from the pricey seafood counter. Next he stopped at the wine area, where he browsed the champagne choices. Ricky maneuvered his cart to the red wine section a few feet away, affording him an unobstructed view. The guy frowned as he picked up the bottles and scrutinized the labels. Finally, he smiled, put a bottle in his cart, and repeated the process a couple more times.

After he left the wine area, Ricky shot over to check the prices of the bottles the man had selected. *No doubt now.* The jackass was making a special dinner, and he could fill in the blank for whom.

Ricky watched him check out and gather up his groceries, using the store's cloth market bags—the ones with the sturdy handles that you had to purchase for a couple dollars each. *No ordinary plastic bags for this splendid asshole.*

Ricky abandoned his full cart at the front of the store and followed the guy outside. He 'accidentally' brushed into him as he walked by, the physical contact sparking his simmering anger. *My work's cut out for me tonight. Enjoy your meal with my wife, dickhead.*

Jack checked his watch—7:30. He ticked through his last-minute list: cheese and grapes, chilled champagne, candles on the table. It'd been a long time since he felt this excited about a date, and he aimed for perfection. Nothing was too good, and the grocery bill proved it. French wines, local greens, shrimp and Caribbean lobster tails: all the makings for an elegant dinner.

He favored intuitive cooking, relying on his internal culinary compass rather than a recipe. When he returned from the market he dove headlong into food prep, enjoying the creative process and the time it gave him to think.

The strange beach incident left him feeling a bit concerned. He wondered who—or why anyone—would go to the trouble of bothering them. *So passive-aggressive. Bribing little kids to carry out a silly prank.*

He'd discussed it with Jessica on their drive back to the condo, but they couldn't come up with an explanation. Jack wondered if Alejandro had a hand in it, but the kids said a man had approached them, not a pirate, let alone a ghost.

Jack started on the salad, chopping cucumbers, slicing tomatoes, tearing leaf lettuce. He'd saved the best thoughts for last. His strong attraction to Jessica surprised him, especially so soon after Rachel. But they shared a significant experience—they attended the same university. He allowed himself to fantasize, picturing the two of them seated at Spartan Stadium watching a football game, or at Jenison Field House watching basketball. He paused from his chopping. *Love at first sight?* The phrase took on some weight and lodged in his brain.

Satisfied dinner was in order, he lit candles, iced the champagne, and selected a soft jazz playlist. His only worry was Jessica's ring. Anxiety dripped, like a leaky faucet, in his mind. *If I can hold off until Alejandro shows up, he'll confess to taking it, and he can give it back to her. If he doesn't show, I'll have to give her the ring and hope she believes I had nothing to do with it.* He shook his head, trying to clear his mind, and glanced once more at his watch—7:45.

Antsy with nervous energy, he decided to have another look at the ring. *Had this thing for twelve hours, and it's caused me a week's worth of worry.* He opened the dresser drawer and ran his hands through the folded clothing. Nothing. He pulled out a shirt and shook it. Nothing. *What the hell? I distinctly remember putting it here.* He yanked out the drawer, dumped the contents on the bed, and dug through the jumbled mess like a hound after a burrowed rabbit, but no ring emerged. *Shit. Shit. Shit. Where is it?*

A knock at the door interrupted his search. Anticipation and dread waged an internal war. He'd been so eager to see Jessica, but the now twice-missing ring put a serious wrinkle in the evening. *Damned Alejandro. Why can't I just have a normal date? Or vacation?*

He took a deep breath and flung the door open. His angst

eased as he took in Jessica's appearance. A pink and white print strapless cotton dress hugged her curves. Her hair, swept into a tousled up-do secured by a feathered clip, revealed the graceful curve of her neck. He couldn't help but smile and stare, the endorphin rush elbowing aside his stress.

Jessica tilted her head and asked, "Well, are you gonna stare or ask me in?"

"*Entrer, cherie.*" Jack bowed at the waist with a grand gesture, sweeping her into an embrace as she stepped inside.

She chuckled and spoke softly in his ear, "You really know how to make a girl feel welcome."

He held her close. "You're so beautiful. I couldn't wait to see you. The Mudslide lunch didn't last nearly long enough, to say nothing of the *beachus interruptus.*"

She leaned back and rested her hands on his arms, scrutinizing his face as if perusing his thoughts. "True confessions, Jack?" A little smile lurked in her eyes.

"Do tell."

"I counted every minute until I could see you again."

"Hmm…that's good. I was concerned you were here just to see the ghost."

A playful gleam lit up her eyes. "I'll admit seeing Alejandro is a powerful draw, but I prefer my men in flesh-and-blood form. There was also the promise of a home-cooked dinner."

He chuckled and kissed her cheek.

His attraction to her was such that he thought he'd burst. His hand slid down to the hollow of her back to press her even closer. He whispered, "How 'bout some champagne?"

She smiled up at him. "Bubbles for my bubbles."

"What?" He raised his eyebrows.

"I'd love some bubbles to go with the bubbles in my stomach."

"I have just the thing." He grinned, took her hand, and led her into the kitchen.

"Wow. Champagne on ice. Romantic music and candles. Impressive, Jack."

He took the bottle of champagne from the ice bucket, wiped off the condensation with a cotton towel, and showed her the label. "Does *Madame* approve?"

Jessica examined the label. "Hmm … Krug Grand Cuvee?" Her eyes sparkled in the candlelight. "*Madame* approves and is very impressed. Proceed with the uncorking, *Monsieur*."

Jack wished time would slow to a crawl so he could savor every minute detail of the evening. After the pop of the cork and rush of bubbles, he filled two champagne flutes and handed one to her.

They entwined their arms and locked gazes. Jack tapped her glass with his in a toast. "To Caribbean nights with a beautiful woman."

A fraction of a second later, his bedroom eyes nearly popped out of their sockets. There, just a couple inches away from his nose, Jessica's right hand clutched the champagne flute, her opal and diamond ring glimmering in the candlelight.

Jack felt like he'd been transported to a slow-motion *Twilight Zone* universe. His confused brain struggled to catch up with the glorious reality as he stared at the ring. *Thank God, it's back!* He swallowed a bit of the champagne and tore his gaze from the ring to Jessica's face.

She wore a puzzled expression as she untangled her arm from his. "Are you okay, Jack? You look, um, perplexed."

"Me? No. I'm fine. In fact, I've never been better."

"What are you staring at?"

"That's the ring you were wearing last night?"

"Yes. You commented on it at the bar." She held her hand out and squinted at the ring. "Anything wrong with it?"

"No. Not at all. Reminds me of a ring my mother wears." The lie made his face heat up. "Hey, I need to take care of some details for dinner. Have a look around, and I'll join you in a minute."

"Sounds good. I'll be on the screened-in porch." She reached up and patted his cheek. "I never had a man cook for me before…very sexy."

"If you keep flirting, you'll never see the meal. Now, go."

As soon as Jessica left the kitchen, Jack slumped against the refrigerator, relief flooding in as the stress drained out. *How the hell did that ring get back to her? Who cares? It's back where it belongs. Damned ghost and his tricks. Wonder if he'll show up tonight?*

Jack closed his eyes. For someone accustomed to being on an even emotional keel, he'd been on a roller coaster the last several months. *Jilted, haunted, and an unwitting party in a jewel heist.*

The strong aroma of pipe smoke penetrated his thoughts. Jack opened his eyes to see a misty cloud seeping into the kitchen through the open window. It twirled around, like a tornado, before gradually resolving into Alejandro's now-familiar figure.

Before the ghost was fully formed, Jack hissed, "Are ya trying to kill me or what? The stress of this damned ring…"

Alejandro emerged from the mist, frowned, and grabbed his cutlass. "Watch yer attitude, ya ungrateful rapscallion!"

Jack's hands tightened into fists. "Oh, that's rich. My attitude? And me, ungrateful? What the fuck are you talking about?" He paused, then continued, mimicking the pirate. "Yer the one that stole Jessica's ring, ya thievin' yellow-bellied blowfish."

The ghost waved his weapon in front of Jack's face, his eyes flashing red. "Stop flappin' yer gums for five seconds, or I'll cut ya into bits and feed yer whinin' arse to th' sharks. And if yer gonna talk like a pirate, study up, ya addled dullard. Should go 'yellow-bellied, bilge swillin' rat.' Blowfish ain't yellow-bellied."

"Great. A grammar lesson from a ghost."

Alejandro tucked the cutlass back under his belt. "Don't appreciate ya accusin' me of high crimes, ya ignorant scoundrel. In me day, stealin' would get ya twenty lashin's of th' cat." He cocked his scarred eyebrow. "I ain't no thief."

Jack huffed. "Bullshit. I woke up this morning, and Jessica's ring was on my bedside stand. I hid it in my drawer, and now it's on her hand. How do you explain that?"

The pirate cupped his ear. "Ya could just skip yer bluster and say, '*Gracias,* Alejandro.'"

"What? Why would I thank you? You got me into this mess."

"Ya daft fool. This ol' shaggy pirate got ya outta this mess." The ghost poked himself in the chest with his thumb. "Th' ring's back on Jessica's finger 'cuz of me."

Jack narrowed his eyes, thoroughly agitated. "Then who stole the fucking ring, Alejandro?"

The pirate lowered his voice. "Ya gots bigger problems than me. Keep a sharp eye out, matey. Gotta go."

The ghost vanished in a mist-like puff, leaving Jack even more perplexed. *What the hell's he talking about? Wish he'd just tell me what he knows. This cryptic crap is driving me crazy.*

Relieved about the ring, Jack returned to the tasks at hand. Rummaging around in the cupboard, he found a couple of pots for boiling the shrimp and lobster. *All set. Better check on Jessica.* He grabbed the champagne and the matches.

Jack found her on the porch, gazing into the night. The twinkling lights of the resort illuminated the white foam of the waves rolling into shore. The sight of her shape in the semi-darkness made his heart thump. "Enjoying the view?"

She answered without turning around. "I never tire of watching the ocean. It's even better with champagne and a handsome man."

"So happens I brought more champagne with me, but I'm sorry, I don't know where to find a handsome man." He set the bottle on the table, struck a match, lit the candles, came up behind her and put his arms around her.

She snuggled into his embrace, leaning her head against his chest. "You're pretty yummy. I think you'll do."

Picking at the edges of his bliss was his old friend, Practicality. *Do you really want a long-distance romance?* But love at first sight now had a voice: *You deserve to be happy.*

Passion and desire did a slow dance in his heart. "Jessica, you're making me crazy."

She whispered, "Good crazy or bad crazy?"

Jack turned her around to face him. She tilted her head back, and he saw desire in her gaze. "Good crazy, Jessica—all good."

The tiniest of smiles touched her lips. She traced his jawline with her finger, barely touching him. He absorbed every detail of her until his senses were strained, tight as violin strings. Her arched eyebrows accented her deep brown eyes, and the natural fragrance from her skin mixed with the barest hint of champagne on her breath.

Jessica closed her eyes, issuing a silent invitation. He accepted and pressed his lips against hers. She placed her hand behind his head, caressing the curls brushing his collar. The intimate gesture fed his passion. Their tongues lightly touched. Jessica wrapped her arms around his shoulders and pressed into him.

The pending dinner flitted through his head. He murmured, "Hey there, sweet pea. How about that dinner I promised you?"

Jessica whispered in his ear, "How 'bout an appetizer first?"

"Hey... I can't have you thinking I invited you here, you know, just for..."

"I don't think that. You're not the scheming type. It's just..." She paused, and rested her hand on his chest.

"Go ahead..."

"It just feels right—doesn't have to be complicated."

It was all he needed to hear. He scooped her up in his arms and carried her into the bedroom. The messy mound of clothes, still on the bed after his frantic search for the ring, caught him off-guard. *A real buzzkill, Romeo. She'll think you're a slob.* He set her down and swept the pile on the floor with one motion.

A smile tugged at her mouth. "Hard time figuring out what to wear tonight?"

Caught between embarrassment and guilt, his face flushed. He muttered, "Something like that."

She grinned and reached for him. "We'll discuss your housekeeping skills later. Now, how 'bout that appetizer?"

– 11 –

Dinner and a Ghost

Jack emerged from a love-stupor, feeling dreamily comfortable with Jessica's head resting on his chest and her arm draped across his shoulder. He ached to blurt out that he loved her, but his gut told him it was too soon. Instead, he kissed the top of her head and hugged her.

She lifted her head and met his gaze, her sultry dark eyes heavy-lidded. She smiled and murmured, "Hey, you."

He turned to his side and pulled her close in a spooning position. "You're full of surprises."

Jessica giggled softly. "Me? Look who's talking. You swept me off my feet while I was minding my own business."

"I blame it on your extreme cuteness, and I really don't believe for a minute you were minding your own business." He nudged her foot with his and grinned.

She turned and faced him. "So, what does all this mean?"

Jack's grin faded as he pondered the serious question, finally going for the bold truth. "For me, it means I haven't felt this way in, well, like ever."

"You were engaged."

"Doesn't mean I was happy." He caressed her cheek with his thumb. "You light me up, Jessica. Now, tell me. What's all this mean to *you*?"

"More than I thought it would."

"Go on..."

"I feel a strong connection with you. That's it, pure and simple." She paused. "I haven't been with anyone since Ricky. After we split, I threw myself into my work. It kept me busy, with no time to think about my failed marriage. How about you? Anyone since your fiancée?"

"No. It's not been that long, but the thought of entering the dating scene again... well, it felt overwhelming. And now there's you. You're so easy to be with."

She threw one leg over his hip, urging him closer, teasing his lips with feathery kisses. "Looking for another appetizer?" whispered Jack.

"Not so fast. I think you promised me dinner." She kissed his nose.

He loved her playful manner, so different from Rachel, who seemed to be perpetually moody. "I tried to feed you earlier, but your other appetite got in the way."

Jessica playfully slapped his arm. "Very funny. Did I see lobster and shrimp in the kitchen?"

"You did. And there's a salad in the fridge."

"Ooh, fancy! Sounds delicious—I'm starving."

"I'll get to work. There's a guest-robe in the closet. Help yourself." He reluctantly disentangled himself.

A butter-drenched piece of lobster dangled from Jessica's fork. "You're an amazing cook, Jack." She popped the morsel into her mouth, dribbling some of the butter on her robe. "Absolutely delicious. What other talents do you have?"

"I can change light bulbs." He smiled.

"Hmmm. I appreciate a handyman. One other talent comes to mind." She grinned a naughty grin, her eyes flashing in the candlelight.

"Oh, you must mean my baking skills. I make a wicked-good dessert, which *you* had before dinner."

She stared at him in mock horror. "You told me that was an appetizer."

"I lied." He winked.

Jessica wore the fluffy white robe loosely belted, revealing the rounded tops of her breasts. He suspected she'd done it just for him, and the notion warmed him to the core.

With Jessica, he experienced a strong emotional closeness, unlike anything he'd known with a partner before. *Is this love? Am I living a cliché?* He felt a squeeze of anxiety in his chest. *Less than forty-eight hours left on the island—then what?* He pushed the troubling thought aside.

She wrinkled her nose. "Do you smell that?"

"Your wish is coming true." He braced himself for the abrupt change of the evening's romantic mood. "The pipe smoke is Alejandro's calling card. He's about to join our little dinner party." He gestured toward the kitchen window. "Watch."

A white mist curled into the room from the open window. As usual, it began to swirl until it moved like a miniature tornado, gathering speed as it took shape.

Jessica sucked in her breath. Her eyes widened. She clutched the robe lapels together at her neck. "Oh, my God! It's really happening!"

Jack took her hand and smiled. "Get ready. He's what you'd call one of a kind." In spite of his reassuring demeanor, he felt a bit uneasy, as Alejandro had proven to be an unpredictable rogue.

The fierce mini-twister revealed the ghost bit-by-bit. Jack watched Jessica's reaction as the tri-cornered hat materialized first, followed by shaggy black hair, piercing dark eyes, and the eyebrow scar. When the image of the pirate was complete, Jessica let out a little squeal.

The ghost struck a pose with attitude—legs in a wide

stance, arms akimbo, pipe clenched between his checkerboard teeth. "Ahoy, Jack me mate! Been too long—haven't seen ye fer…" He pulled a gold watch from his vest pocket and held it at arm's length, squinting. "Eyesight ain't what it used to was…uh, been twenty-four hours."

"That long, huh?" He sighed, relieved that the ghost didn't admit to their brief encounter a couple of hours ago.

The pirate raised his eyebrows and shifted his attention to Jessica. With a dramatic gesture, he doffed his hat and held it over his heart. "Ah, Jessica me beauty, yer a sight fer these ancient eyes. A scabby-arsed scalawag like meself is unfit to be in th' presence of such allurement."

He floated toward her, attempting to pick up her hand as if to kiss it, but to no avail. His hand passed through hers. "Avast! Used up all me energy last night kickin' arse on th' beach. Can't even pick up th' lovely lady's hand." He wiggled his fingers and arched his eyebrows. "Ye'll have to be happy feastin' on me good looks wit' yer eyes."

"You're the real deal, aren't you? You're a duppy." She reached out to touch the ghost, but her hand just passed through thin air.

"Aaaar, get yer hand out of me kidneys!"

She snapped her hand back to her side, her eyes as large as banjos. "S—s—sorry."

Alejandro snorted with laughter. "No worries, me dear; jus' fuckin' wit' ya."

Jack shook his head. "Nice talk. I know you're a pirate, but can you watch your language around the lady?"

"It's okay, Jack," said Jessica. "We should thank Alejandro for coming to our rescue on the beach last night."

"A good fight a'ways scratches me itch." The pirate grinned and patted the brass hilt of his cutlass. "Haven't had 'at much fun in a hundred yar." He waggled his eyebrows and leaned in toward Jessica. "Damsels in distress is me specialty."

She laughed, clearly entertained by Alejandro's ghostly

nonsense. "So, you've been hanging around this island for quite some time, haven't you?"

"Ah, me sweet, o'er three hundred yar."

"Why?" Jessica shrugged.

He arched one eyebrow. "Maybe 'tis none of yer business." He tucked his hand between the buttons of his blousy shirt, affecting an air of indifference, and looked toward the ceiling. "Maybe me likes it here."

"Alejandro's time on this island is limited," said Jack. "In fact, he has to cross over in just a couple of days."

Jessica frowned. "Cross over?"

Jack whispered, "To the other side."

The ghost glared at Jack. "Ye know, I can hear ye." He gestured in Jessica's direction. "Got me cross-over orders. No choice. Gotta go."

She nodded. "So your haunting days are over?"

"That's a bad word." The ghost huffed and crossed his arms.

"What's a bad word?"

He stage-whispered, "Haunting—bad word. We half-perished spirits use th' word 'surveillance.'"

Jessica made the air-quote gesture. "Like you 'surveilled' that inn on the beach for years?"

"Huh. Scurvy bastards shuttered th' place. Been driftin' ever since."

Jack interrupted, impatient for his long-awaited explanation. "Why are you here now? I fulfilled my promise. One night on the town—took you to the beach bar last night, which didn't turn out so well ..."

"Quit yer carpin', ya lily-livered pansy. Ye best be thankin' me. I made ye a hero." The ghost cupped his ear with his hand, an expectant expression on his face.

"Okay, okay." Jack pursed his lips. "Thanks for the exciting but dangerous evening, Alejandro."

"Ye needed some excitement in yer borin' life. An' what's dangerous? 'Twas th' drunken bilge rat that had a meal o' yer fist. Ye surprised this ol' pirate—didn't think ye had th' stones to bust up his nose." His voice dropped to a whisper. "Wenches love a bloke 'at can hold his own in a fight."

Jessica laughed. "You sure know how to put a spin on a story, Alejandro."

The pirate winked at Jessica and turned toward Jack. "Then thar's 'at wee matter o' me comin' to yer rescue when th' second lard-brain drunk showed up. A'most skewered his gizzard." He put his hand over his heart. "But, no need t' thank me fer that one." The ghost smiled and pointed at Jack. "Ye jus' owes me another favor."

Jack bolted from his chair. "So that's why you came back tonight. You want something. Why doesn't that surprise me? Well, forget it. I'm done with your ghost games." Jack poked his chest with his thumb. "I'm the one that's supposed to be relaxing on vacation, not playing escort to a deceased pirate."

Jessica stood and took Jack's arm. "It can't hurt to hear his request. Maybe it's something easy. After all, he did help us out of a bad situation last night."

"Thar's a girl after me own heart." Alejandro shot Jack a wounded look and wafted over to Jessica, wiping at the transparent tears glistening on his rugged face. "Aah, yer jus' like yer great-great-great-great-great-great-great-grandma. Ye have th' same smile and sassy ways. Sweet, kind, 'n always lookin' fer th' next adventure."

"My how-many-greats grandma?" She furrowed her brow. "What's she have to do with anything? Did you know her?"

"Blimey! That's a long story, me beauty. I'll git to it, but first, we need to square away that favor ya owes me."

Jessica fixed her gaze on the pirate. "You seem really, um ... advanced for a ghost. Almost too real. It's like I'm talking to a live person, except I can see through you. Are you one hundred percent dead?"

"Dead as the lobster ya just ate." Alejandro chuckled. "'Tis me spirit that's lively. Ya see, they granted me extry powers for me last few days." The pirate pointed toward the ceiling. "Some picaroon from up there sent me the message, 'Go big before ya go home.' What's 'at supposed ta mean?"

Jessica laughed. "The phrase is, 'Go big or go home.' Sounds like the afterlife has a sense of humor. So, now you have more abilities than you did before?"

"Aye. Me image and me energy is stronger, and..." he winked, "I'm more handsome." The ghost lit his pipe and took a couple mighty puffs, squinting through the gray-tinged smoke. "Now, how 'bout that favor?"

– 12 –

Another Favor

Jack's patience started wearing thin with the ghost, but with Jessica hanging on his arm, he rallied and asked, "Okay, Alejandro, what's your next demand? Lucky for you, Jessica's intrigued by your connection to her long-ago grandmother."

Alejandro grinned, flaunting his cocky attitude. "Always been a ladies' man. Th' young damsels can't resist a swarthy pirate."

Jessica giggled.

"Don't encourage him," Jack muttered. He peered at the ghost. "Enough swashbuckling. What do you want?"

The pirate sighed; his transparent image quivered from the effort. "I be longin' to board th' big ship afore me crosses over."

Jack and Jessica exchanged puzzled glances and asked simultaneously, "What big ship?"

Alejandro shook his head in mock dismay. "Just one night o' rompin' and a'ready yer talkin' fer each other." He pointed to his head. "Are both o' ye daft? Them big ships 'r here all th' time. Sometimes all stacked up in th' harbor."

Jessica nodded. "Oh, you mean a cruise ship?"

"Don't care what ya call 'em, just want me a look-see before I hafta go—me last chance." He slouched and looked at them with puppy dog eyes. "Been yearnin' fer me ol' pirate ship; a splendid sloop she was, till that flea-bit, bilge suckin' Blackbeard sunk 'er. Plundered me treasures 'n blew 'er to smithereens wit' cannonballs."

"You *knew* Blackbeard?" In spite of trying to maintain an indifferent attitude, Jack's demeanor cracked. "I love Blackbeard stories. As a kid, I read anything about him that I could get my hands on."

"Aye. I knew 'im." Alejandro perked up, and the sparkle came back into his eyes. He lowered his voice. "A mean bunghole he was too—soul murky as a swamp." He glanced at the two and hung his head. "Ah, but ye don't want t' hear me tellin' sorry tales from so long ago."

"Yes, we do…don't we?" Jessica nudged Jack with her elbow. "This is exciting stuff. I mean, just think—he knew Blackbeard!"

Jack took a deep breath. *Here we go. Jessica's infatuated with the ghost and his tales, which means I'll get roped into doing something to help him because I'm infatuated with Jessica.*

"If Blackbeard stole your treasure and sunk your ship, why didn't he kill you?" Jack frowned, suspicious of the pirate's story. "Or maybe he did kill you, and that's when you became a ghost?"

"Let me tell ya 'bout Blackbeard." Alejandro nodded and took a puff of his pipe. "A strappin' man he was. Thick beard, black as midnight, 'at grew clear up to 'is eyes. Pirates 'n' sailors—'fraid of their own shadows—swore he was th' spawn of th' devil. Said sparks and smoke billowed from 'is head like he'd crawled up from th' bowels of hell." Alejandro tapped his forehead. "He was a smart bastard and messed wit' yer head. Ya see, he was a trickster—tucked hemp cords under 'is hat, then set 'em afire—slow burnin' and smoky, a fierce sight."

"How'd you escape?" asked Jack.

Alejandro's eyes flickered. "Blackbeard's men scuttled me ship wit' a cannonball, and then scrambled aboard, like filthy bilge rats. Ran me cutlass through a couple, but there were too many of 'em. We lost th' battle, and th' thievin' blighters held me against th' mast at sword point."

"You killed two men?" asked Jessica.

"Avast! They had it comin'." The ghost's eyes narrowed as he relived the moment. "Blackbeard boarded last, head a-smokin' and armed to th' teeth—daggers tucked in 'is black boots and a wicked cutlass by 'is side. He drew a blunderbuss and held it against me skull."

"Blunderbuss?" asked Jack.

"A nasty lookin' long pistol wit' a flared end. At close range there'd be nothin' left of me brains." A little flame, that came from no visible source, appeared in the ghost's pipe. The smell of tobacco intensified as he continued his story. "Blackbeard sneered and yelled, 'Hand over yer ship, ya son of a whore.' We wuz loaded with Cuban rum. Liquid gold, ya see. Ta hell and be damned—I spat in 'is face and told 'im to go to th' fiery depths o' Hades."

Alejandro paused and drifted closer to Jessica. "See th' scar on me face? He told me shootin' was too good for me. So, th' bastard cut me wit' his cutlass. Called me a wretched heap o' shark bait, and threw me overboard. A long way from shore, we were. He laughed and bellowed at me t' swim for me life. At th' time, I wished he'd blown me head off instead, for th' blood was drippin' in me eyes; me death would surely be a drownin' one, or a blood-hungry shark would have me fer 'is supper. But a sea turtle, th' size of a rum barrel, swam up beside me… like she was guidin' me inta shore. I hung onto 'er shell. Me will t' live and that loggerhead delivered me t' land."

"Oh, my God!" said Jessica. "You poor thing. Injured and no ship. What happened when you reached the shore?"

The ghost made a sweeping gesture, like an affected movie director.

"Picture this, me sweet. I was th' spittin' image of a drowned bilge rat, face-down bleedin' in th' sand, gaspin' fer breath; watchin' me ship sink under th' waves. Rubbed me eyes wit' me ragged 'n' filthy sleeve, then looked up to see a vision of loveliness standin' over me."

A stickler for details, Jack broke into the story. "What year was this?"

"Ye're interruptin' th' flow of me story, ya screw-eyed bird-brain." Alejandro frowned and shot him a perturbed look. "'Twas 1715."

"Three hundred years ago—amazing—and Blackbeard died in 1718. You're a genuine piece of history."

"Aye. Maybe now ye'll treat me wit' a bit more respect. Now, let's talk about boardin' th' big ship."

Jessica made the time-out gesture. "Hold on, Alejandro. Who was that vision of loveliness?"

"Th' most beautiful woman this Earth 'as ever seen." The ghost put his hand over his heart and looked directly at Jessica, his dark eyes glinting in the candlelight. "The love of me life, Rose Bodden. Yer direct ancestor, young lady."

"Is she the many-times-great grandmother you mentioned?" She frowned and continued, "Wait. If that happened in 1715, she'd be my..."

"Yer gettin' picky. Time don't mean much t' ghosts. Rose was yer long-ago grandmother. That's all ye need t' know."

"Oh my God! Does that mean you're my long-ago grandfather?"

"Yer gettin' ahead o' th' story, Missy. I'll git t' that, but first we need t' settle up me gittin' a look-see at th' big ship."

Jack shook his head. "You don't need me for that. Just float, levitate, or whatever you ghosts do, out to the ship. You can go anywhere, and nobody can see you."

"Ye don't know nothin'." Alejandro folded his arms across his chest and harrumphed. "Can't leave th' island."

"Why not? What's stopping you?"

"Me contract."

"What are you talking about?"

"Didn't want t' cross over when I kicked th' bucket." He pointed to the ceiling. "So they gave me a three hundred yar lease on this island. Can't leave land unless me hitches a ride."

Jessica piped up. "Why didn't you want to cross over when you died?"

"Had me a job to do. Couldn't leave."

"What job?"

The ghost lifted his hands to the heavens in a show of exasperation. "Enough questions!"

Jack rolled his eyes at Alejandro's theatrics. "Hope this question doesn't push you over the edge—how does a ghost 'hitch a ride,' exactly?"

"Like this." The pirate's eyes twinkled, his pleased look indicating Jack had taken the bait he'd so skillfully tossed out.

In a heartbeat, the ghost vanished and reappeared, superimposed on Jack.

Jack stumbled from the unexpected weight. "Hey, what are ya doing? Get off me! You're heavy."

"Quit whinin', ya ninny. Ye'll get used to me. See? We'll walk on th' ship together. After that, I can be on me own. Go ahead—take a few steps."

Jack, bent over from the extra poundage, stumbled forward a few steps. "Can't you make yourself lighter? I can barely lift your hefty ass."

Jessica snorted and laughed. "You two are ridiculous!"

Alejandro called out, "Catch this!" His right hand materialized holding his cutlass, and he flung it at Jessica. She shrieked and ducked as the diaphanous weapon hurtled toward her, disappearing into thin air mere inches from her head.

"Much better." Jack straightened. "What'd you do?"

"Got rid of me cutlass." The ghost floated away from Jack's body and settled next to Jessica, his image wavering in the ceiling fan's breeze.

"Your sword weighs that much?"

"Weaponry 'tis a burdensome load, me friend. Not wise fer me t' be unarmed, but ye ain't strong enough t' carry me wit' it."

"I'll loan you my Swiss Army knife. You can slice your way through the cruise ship with that."

"Now yer talkin'." Alejandro clapped his hands together. "Let's go!"

Jessica poured more champagne into her glass and took a sip. "I hate to throw a bucket of cold reality on your dream, Alejandro, but you can't just walk onto a cruise ship."

"Why th' hell not?"

"Security." She pointed her champagne flute in the ghost's direction, sloshing some on the table. "You need a passenger identification card to board the ship. Jack doesn't have that."

Jack brightened at the prospect of aborting the cruise ship plan. "See, Alejandro? It won't work. Too many obstacles."

"I have an idea that just might work, though." Jessica squinted, deep in thought.

"I think the whole thing's a bad idea." Jack frowned. "Plus, I have no desire to go on a cruise ship."

"Let th' young wench speak, ya ill-mannered oaf."

"I have a friend—well, acquaintance, really—a cruise director on the ship called *Island Queen*. Last year, I housed a couple of her passengers in a rental condo due to a medical emergency. Marcy told me she owed me a favor."

"What's that got to do with me gaining access to the cruise ship?" asked Jack.

"Her ship comes in every two weeks. Tomorrow is the day. I'll text Marcy and tell her my friend, a businessman, is interested in touring the *Island Queen*, researching the possibility of a Caribbean cruise reward trip for his sales reps." Jessica's eyes brightened. "It's perfect. You'll have an escort, a guided tour—everything on the up-and-up, and Alejandro gets his last request before *permanently* crossing over."

"Sounds like the champagne talking, Jessica."

"Aye—give th' wench some more. I like 'er a bit tipsy. Things are lookin' up for this ol' scraggly pirate."

Jessica stared at the ghost. "If we get you on the ship, will you tell me the rest of my family's story?"

"Aye. Never could say no to a comely wench like yerself. I'm a man of me word."

Jack guffawed. "You most certainly are *not* a man of your word. You told me one favor, and you'd be gone. You're still here, and now we're working on the second favor. And, why me? Why am I 'the one?'"

The ghost's eyes twinkled. "Why ye? Truth be told, ya remind me of me brother, Javier—a batten-down-the-hatches kinda bloke." The pirate winked. "Gotta admit, this scabby ol' salt 'as put some adventure in yer life. Sometimes, Jack, ya need ta ride th' storm."

Jessica threw her arms around Jack's neck. "Ah, do him a favor. After all, it's Alejandro's last chance before he crosses over. The tour should only take about an hour or so. Easy peasy. It might even be fun."

"I'll take him on the ship, but only so you can learn the history of your ancestors." He gathered her into a hug. "I'm doing this for you."

"Thanks, Jack." She flashed a heart-melting smile. "And, really, where's the harm in a little tour?"

– 13 –

Ricky the Menace

Alejandro celebrated his victory by dancing a little pirate-y jig. "I got me a big ship now!"

"You don't 'got' any ship," said Jessica. "Remember, you're along for the ride with Jack. The cruise ships usually leave port around four in the afternoon. That means your tour will occur earlier in the day; that is, if my friend's available to give a tour." She paused, wearing a quizzical expression. "Are ghosts available in the daylight hours?"

The pirate abruptly stopped dancing, his face a picture of dejection. "Whaddaya mean *if* yer friend be available?" He scowled and smacked his fist on his chest. "This ol' salt be countin' on it. Ye promised."

"Remember *we're* doing *you* a favor." Jack frowned in exasperation.

"I didn't promise you anything, mister." Jessica's tone was scolding, like a parent to a naughty child. "If the tour is a 'go,' how do we reach you?"

"Ye only has t' say me name." With that, Alejandro winked and spun himself, like a mini-tornado, out the window.

The two stared at the wisp of ghostly vapor hanging in the air. Jack draped his arm around Jessica's shoulders. "I realize duppies are part of the Caribbean culture, but does it strike you as somewhat incredible that we just negotiated with a *ghost* for almost an hour?"

"It's a first for me," said Jessica. "If you ever wanted a peek behind the curtain, you got one tonight. I mean, who knew… contracts from and with the afterlife?"

"Makes you wonder. Does everyone negotiate a contract when they die?"

"Very bizarre." She snuggled into him, putting her arms around his waist. "I don't know if I should feel privileged or scared. He was a little testy just before he disappeared."

"I agree." Jack tapped his watch. "Hey, it's been a long day, and it's late. I'm assuming you're working tomorrow and need your sleep."

She stepped away from his embrace. "Yes, to both. I'd better go back upstairs to my place. My cat probably wonders where I've been."

"I love spending time with you, Jessica." He caught her hand and paused, then decided to forge ahead. "If you like, well… please stay the night."

A tender smile brightened her face. "Oh, Jack. I feel the same. I'm a little freaked out by Alejandro. I'd love to stay."

He pulled her into his arms and kissed her forehead. "I'll protect you from all the duppies on this island."

"It's a deal." Jessica yawned. "I'm going to bed. Very tired."

"Go ahead. I'll be there in a minute." He watched her stroll down the hall, the large robe obscuring her petite figure, and smiled.

He stacked the dinner dishes and took them into the kitchen. *Don't want her to wake up to a mess and think I'm a slob.* An image of the jumbled pile of clothes on the bedroom floor whizzed through his mind. *Probably already thinks that.*

While loading the dishwasher, Jack mulled over the incredible events of the last few days. *I'm living an adventure. Ghosts and romance in the Caribbean. Maybe that ridiculous pirate had a point—maybe I needed to shake up my life.*

He turned off lights and blew out candles as he made his way to the bedroom. Jessica's rhythmic breathing reminded him of his own fatigue. He snuck under the covers, relishing the intimacy of sharing his bed with someone so special, and drifted into a dreamless sleep.

Ricky pressed the binoculars tight to his face, straining to see whatever he could in the darkness. For the last hour, he'd spied on Jessica and her boyfriend. He leaned up against the adjacent building, obscured by the bougainvillea plants. Bad enough Jessica was having a romantic dinner with Mr. Wonderful, but now it was midnight. All lights were off, and she hadn't left to walk up the stairs to her condo. Which could mean only one thing: a sleepover.

Cheating whore. Perhaps he'd relied too much on their families' friendship serving as the glue of their marriage. At times, he'd felt his own mother preferred Jessica to him, her only son, indeed her only child. She'd joked, "No matter what happens between you and Jessica, we're keeping her." *Nice.*

He sighed. High school had been the golden years. His mouth formed a bitter smile as he recalled how he and Jessica were in love and having the time of their lives. So many friends, so much fun. The secluded beach by the old haunted inn was their favorite hangout, and they'd spent many days swimming in the Caribbean and building beach fires at night. But then Jessica, the over-achiever, decided to go to college in the US. The University College on the island wasn't good enough for her. *No sir.* She had to go all the way to fucking Michigan to learn how to keep assholes happy on their vacations. *Hospitality degree, my ass.*

Before she left for college, he'd extracted a promise from her to come back to him. Undeniably, one of his proudest moments. Unable to keep tabs on her from afar, her commitment to him became the next best thing. Hell, he'd even sprung for a ring to seal the deal. Not a diamond—way beyond his budget, but a plain silver band engraved with a heart. His mother, kill-joy that she was, had frowned at the fifty-dollar trinket and warned him not to put Jessica in a box, that she needed room to grow. *Gee Mom, thanks one fuck of a lot for being on my side.*

While Jessica was gone, he contented himself working part-time for a lawn service company and hanging out at the beach with his leftover high school buddies. Realizing he'd have to eventually work for a living, he finally enrolled in the Fundamentals of Construction curriculum at the local University College. One semester into the program, it became clear to him there were way too many rules and restrictions in that line of work. He'd regularly dozed through the Building Regulation and Specifications class, and from there it went downhill. He flunked out; but, to him, it felt like reclaiming his freedom.

By the time Jessica returned from college, he was working for a pool cleaning company. She seemed happy to pick up where they left off. Indeed, his instincts affirmed that she was still hot for him. He brought his "A" game to the sack. You couldn't fake great sex like what he doled out. He rubbed his stiffening cock at the memory. It must've paid off—because she agreed to marry him.

He had envisioned a cushy life ahead of him, all because Jessica landed a primo job at a boutique hotel. So, he quit the pool cleaning gig. Too many hours, and working with all those pool chemicals couldn't be good. He figured his chief duties were to keep her well-fucked and off his ass. That fantasy burst when she decided he needed a job. Armed with her college degree, she apparently felt qualified to direct his life. It was her idea to start the pool cleaning business. At first, it wasn't all bad. Hell, as the owner of the company, he could work short days and pocket cash from the business. But then, Ms. College Degree declared the business was losing money. He grunted. *Whatever happened to a woman standing by her man?* The marriage took a solid hit. In a cold confrontation, Jessica told him she'd lost respect for him, didn't love him anymore, and to pack his shit and leave. His skin prickled at the memory.

And now, unable and unwilling to accept the divorce, he pulled out the only high card in an otherwise losing hand—the religion card. Yes, in the eyes of the Lord, he was still married. It was right there in the Bible in black ink and plain English. "What God has joined together, let no man put asunder."

Don't you get it, Jessica? We're meant to be together forever. God's will. Ricky's attitude softened for a moment. *She's going through a phase and will come back to me.* An unwelcome vision of her naked and entwined with another man popped into his head. Anger pushed aside any tender thoughts. *She's ruined. Blackened by filthy, lustful sex.*

A muttered string of obscenities tumbled from his mouth. The strong smell of burning tobacco caught his attention and hushed his toxic spewing. He remembered the aroma from the last time he'd hunkered here out of sight. *Fucking old guy's smoking on his porch again.*

Before Ricky could investigate, an unseen force yanked the binoculars from his grasp and slammed the three-hundred-dollar Bushnells against the stucco building. The sound of shattering glass and breaking plastic pierced the night air.

Alarmed, Ricky turned and back-stepped away from the wall, straight into the bougainvillea. He instinctively grabbed at the thick spiky branches for balance and yelped as thorns punctured his hand.

"Who's there?" he called out in what he hoped was a menacing voice.

The wind picked up and stirred the thorny branches, scratching the backs of his legs. A light mist settled on his skin, making him shiver. Suddenly, a craggy voice whispered in his ear, "Get lost, ya slimy maggot."

– 14 –

Breakfast in Bed

The Caribbean sunshine leaked in through the gauzy curtains, plucking Jack from a deep slumber. Peeking out from the veil of delicious sleep, his arm slowly extended, searching the bed for Jessica. Instead of her pleasing body, his exploring hand discovered a slip of paper lying on top of her pillow. The thought of her leaving a note gave him pause. He brought it to his face, trying not to think the worst, and blinked to clear his morning vision.

> *Jack: You looked so cute while you were sleeping, I didn't want to disturb you. Had to feed Carrots and get ready for work. I'll let you know about the cruise ship tour. Loved our night together.*
> *The most exciting date I've ever had.* ❤

He smiled at the hand-drawn heart. *Guess I'm still "in."* An unwelcome fact crept into his mind, like a hairy spider. *Gotta leave tomorrow. Maybe I should extend—change my flight.* A knock interrupted his internal monologue. He got out of bed, pulled on running shorts, and made his way to the door.

Jessica's fresh, smiling face appeared through the peephole. He flung the door open. She held up a coffee carafe and assorted pastries on a plate. "Good morning. Hot coffee and breakfast?"

His heart flip-flopped at the thoughtful gesture—and at the sight of her small frame clad in a short tropical print skirt and white top. "Wow. What a treat! And the breakfast looks great too."

She giggled. "You're such a flirt." She walked into the condo and set the items on the table.

He nabbed her in an embrace and murmured, "You look gorgeous. I just read your note. You snuck out early this morning."

She met his eyes with a fake stern gaze. "*Two* hours ago. And you're just now waking up at what, ten o'clock? Did you party with the island girls late into the night?"

"Only one island girl. A real hottie. She was all I could handle—had her way with me, she did. And then she demanded dinner. Halfway through dinner, a pirate ghost showed up. You can't make this stuff up."

"Poor guy. Maybe I should stay with you the rest of the day to protect you from the dangers of this little island."

He chuckled and whispered, "Excellent idea." He kissed her, kicking the door shut. Jessica's soft, warm mouth parted. Her hands slid inside the elastic waistband of his running shorts and cupped his rear, her thumbs gently caressing his cheeks. Her amorous move flamed his passion.

His desire for her grew white-hot. He cast aside all thought of falling too hard and too fast. When their tongues touched, a thrilling sensation traveled down his spine.

Quickly unbuttoning her blouse, his hands relished the feel of her soft skin as he traced her breasts. Jessica clung to him and nudged him in the direction of the bedroom.

He successfully backed into the room without breaking their kiss. When he bumped into the edge of the bed, he fell back, pulling Jessica on top of him. He unzipped her skirt, and she wiggled out of it, kicking it to the floor. Jack snuck his hand under the flimsy barrier of her thong panties. She gasped as he stroked her.

She whispered, "Hurry. I can't wait much longer."

He twisted free of his only article of clothing. Jessica, seemingly focused on perfecting the art of the quickie, straddled him, joining their bodies in the age-old dance of love. Their simultaneous release was swift. Happiness enveloped Jack like a plush blanket. He clung to the feeling, never wanting it to end.

Jessica stirred first. She tapped on his forehead. "Hey—you in there?"

Jack opened one eye, her flushed face and tousled wavy hair appearing before him like a vision. He said, "Barely."

A little smile played on her face. "Oh, come on. I wasn't that rough on you."

"Really? I never even got to eat my breakfast."

"I'll bring it to you. Don't move."

The bed squeaked as she got up. He watched her put on her skirt and button her blouse, and then closed his eyes. He preferred to stay in la-la land, but a remarkably persistent thought burst through the fog of contentment. *You love her, Jack. No denying it.*

Jessica entered the room with a mug in her hand. "Here's your coffee. And, guess what? It's still hot. That tells you how quick the quickie was."

Jack moved to lean against the bed's headboard, and she put a pillow behind his back. "Comfy?"

He sipped the rich brew, smiled and caressed her cheek. "You're spoiling me."

"You deserve to be spoiled."

"We've gotta talk." He took her hand and kissed it.

"I know. You leave tomorrow morning."

"Well, that's what my airline ticket says."

"Hmm. Are you saying your airline ticket isn't the last word?"

"You're quick on all fronts today, aren't you?"

She put her hands in front of her face. "Should I be embarrassed?"

"Absolutely not." He reached out and drew her close. "I love your zest for life and your playful, lusty ways. I'm falling in love with you, Jessica. It may sound, well, way too soon, but it's true."

Jessica pulled away and stared into Jack's eyes. "I wasn't expecting that."

He tensed, not sure if the declaration of his feelings was welcome. But, detecting warmth in her eyes, he relaxed.

"Oh, Jack. I'm crazy about you, but I just don't know if I can say... I mean, it's such a big step..."

He hugged her and took a deep breath. "It's okay. I'm happy with crazy for now. I had to tell you. I've never connected with any woman like this before. All new territory for me, Jessica. I hope I don't scare you away."

"I'm not so easily scared. If a ghost couldn't manage it, I doubt you can." She cupped his faced and gently kissed him, then dropped her hands onto his shoulders. "Now, about that plane ticket—any chance of extending your stay?"

"I can stay for another couple of days, but then duty calls, and I'll have to go back to Michigan—back to my job."

"I understand. Two more days are better than zero days."

"There's just one problem—I have to vacate this condo by noon tomorrow, which means I have no place to stay."

"Hmm. It happens I know of a condo one floor above this one. The only problem, you'll have to share it with the property manager and her cat."

"I'm an excellent houseguest."

She clapped her hands together. "Done!" She leaned in to kiss him. "In fact, pack your stuff today. Why wait?" She glanced over the edge of the bed and scowled at the mess on the floor. "You'll have to tidy up a bit—I have it on good authority that the property manager doesn't care for clutter."

"Yeah. Well, I'm normally not sloppy. There's a reason for all the clothes on the floor. More about that later."

Her face brightened. "Oh, one more thing. The very reason I came by this morning was to tell you that my friend, Marcy, is willing to give you a tour of the cruise ship. In fact, you have to be there at noon sharp."

He shot Jessica a sideways look. "I don't believe for one minute that was the *very reason* you stopped by. I think you wanted to sample my goodies ... again."

"I guess you'll never know for sure, will you?"

"Oh, believe me, I already know." He shook his head and smirked. "I'd hoped that tour would be a no-go. So, what time is it?" He glanced at the clock on the bedside stand. "Oh no. It's 11:00. I've gotta shower."

He hopped off the bed. "You can be the one to summon Alejandro. After all, he's taken quite a shine to you."

– 15 –

All Aboard!

Showered and dressed, Jack waited as Jessica called out for Alejandro. The ghost appeared in a whirl that gradually resolved into his swashbuckling image, hands gripping a spectral wooden ship's wheel.

"Ahoy, matey!" He turned the wheel back and forth, grinning like a little kid with a new toy. "Can't wait to steer me a ship again. That fargin' Blackbeard can kiss me hairy arse…"

"Don't want to wreck your fantasy, but the ship is tied up at the pier. It's not goin' anywhere." Jack glanced at Jessica and sighed.

"We'll see 'bout that. 'Tis me big day—step lively, buck-o."

Jack hugged Jessica and moved toward the door. "I'll call you when I get back on land. Hopefully, it won't be too long…"

"Marcy's assistant will meet you at the pier and escort you aboard. I noticed a cab outside—take that downtown. No sense walking and working up a sweat." She smiled and kissed him on the cheek. "Hey, you might even decide you want to take a cruise someday."

"Rather be here with you. Wish me luck." He cast a skeptical glance in the ghost's direction. "If Alejandro keeps his promise, we'll hear the story of your ancestors tonight. That'd be more interesting than the tour."

Alejandro nodded, winked, and then snapped his pale fingers. "See ya, matey." He disappeared with a poof.

The cab, lime green and embellished with a pink palm tree decal, rolled to a stop at the curb. Jack emerged from the backseat. Frigid conditioned air escaped from the car to mingle with the hot, humid air of Georgetown. While he paid the driver, a sticky sheen of sweat materialized on his skin.

He took in the downtown scene. On his right, the Caribbean Sea sparkled in bright sunshine; its cobalt blue hue provided a stunning contrast to the gleaming white cruise ship docked at the pier. He gazed at the behemoth tethered by thick ropes and metal cables. Earlier, he'd Googled the *Island Queen* and learned she was nine hundred sixty-four feet long and two hundred feet high. Although built for pleasure, to Jack, it represented a potential floating house of horrors. *Why in the hell did I let myself get talked into this?* He reminded himself that he'd only have to endure the unpredictable ghost for about an hour. Still, a feeling of angst lingered like a hangover. His body released a trickle of sweat down his back.

The cacophony of vehicles and people intruded on his thoughts. He caught a whiff of fried food and observed the traffic-choked street on his left. The usual Caribbean commerce lined the thoroughfare: restaurants, tee shirt shops, perfume and jewelry stores. He smirked at a giant statue of a pirate advertising Big Black Dick's Dark Rum. *Ha! Dead ringer for Alejandro.* The whole downtown scene emitted a gaudy, tacky vibe.

Jack checked his watch and made his way toward the ship. A hopeful thought blossomed. *Maybe Alejandro won't show—he's a couple of minutes late already.* His optimism flattened as an extra twenty pounds of ghostly energy landed on him, pitching him forward.

"Hey! A little warning would've been nice. Can't see you in the daylight."

"Good show, matey! Right on time. Mind if I hitch me a ride?"

Jack sighed and mumbled, "You just did. Like I wasn't hot enough already."

"Hey, lighten up! 'Tis me big moment. A bit o' enthusiasm wouldn't hurt, ya pox-faced landlubber."

Jack shrugged and rolled his shoulders, distributing the ghost's weight evenly across his back. He lumbered toward the cruise ship and seized the opportunity for a last-minute lecture. "Remember, we are *guests* on this boat. Jessica's friend has graciously consented to give *me* a tour. We're here under the guise of research for a business trip. So, none of your pranks."

"Stop yer whinin'. Ye worry like an old woman. What do ya suppose be a pirate's chance o' gettin' laid afore he crosses over?"

"Getting laid? You can't be serious—you're a ghost. I thought you only wanted to board the ship."

"Ships 'n' wenches, matey—me favorites all rolled inta one."

"You're a real piece of work, Alejandro. Who's gonna screw a ghost? Most people can't even see you ..." Jack felt a jab in his side from Alejandro. "Knock it off. What do you think I am, a horse?"

"Button yer gob. See 'at comely wench holdin' th' sign up ahead?"

Jack squinted into the distance and noticed a woman in uniform. "Yes, I see her." As he ambled closer, he read the sign: Welcome Jack Garret.

"Me chances are lookin' up, matey. She could be th' one."

"Stop it. Don't cause any trouble with her or anyone else on this ship. Geez, you're a load. Once we've made the transfer from land to ship, you don't have to be superimposed on me, but that doesn't mean you can roam around as you see fit. Just stick by my side, and don't cause any trouble."

"Thar ya go again, barkin' out orders. 'At's one fine lookin' wench. Maybe she'd like a tour of me britches. Wit' me extry powers she'll be screamin' me name."

Jack pressed his lips together, choosing to ignore Alejandro, and approached the uniformed woman. He frowned. *Wonder why he finds her so 'comely?'* She appeared to be somewhere north of fifty, and practically poured into her uniform. The buttons on her blouse begged for mercy as they pulled against the taut fabric.

She raised the sign in greeting, a big smile on her face. "You must be Jack. Welcome to the *Island Princess.* My name's Francine. I'm Marcy's assistant, and will help you register as our guest. Follow me."

Francine and her hips sashayed up the metal-cleated ramp toward the fourth deck, her sensible gel-soled lace-up shoes making little squeaky noises.

"Aaar! 'At's a fine badunkadunk on 'at strumpet. Ask 'er if she wants to sample me hornpipe."

Hoping the street noise would muffle his words, he muttered through clenched teeth, "Shut up. She's probably someone's grandma, not a 'strumpet,' you dimwitted fool."

"Had t' lower me standards. No time t' be picky. Gotta get laid before me crosses over tomorrow."

To Jack's horror he observed the back of Francine's skirt lifting up, exposing her granny pants and stout thighs. She squealed, yanked the skirt back in place, then whirled around to face Jack, her face thunderous. "What are you up to, mister?"

"Pardon me?" Luckily, Jack's hands were stuffed in his pockets, and he conjured up what he thought would pass for an innocent look on his face.

"You didn't see that?"

"What are you talking about? I was gawking at the ship. What happened?"

She frowned, her anger fading into puzzlement. "My skirt… well, never mind. The wind must've caught it." Shooting Jack a dubious look, she turned and proceeded up the ramp.

More sweat trickled down Jack's back. *Damn it! The very thing I was worried about. Wish I could dump Alejandro's ass overboard.*

He boarded the ship, cleared security, clipped on a guest badge, and attempted small talk with a highly suspicious Francine, who kept her distance while instructing him to wait for Marcy in the security area. Relieved to shed Alejandro's extra weight, he could barely make out the ghostly shape beside him.

As soon as Francine was out of sight, he whispered in the angriest tone he could muster, "I told you, *no pranks*. And what's the very first thing you do—pull up that poor woman's skirt?"

"Stop yer snivelin'. Best thing 'at happened to 'er all day."

Utterly unfazed by Jack's scolding, the pirate launched into excited chatter. "Blow me down! Ever see a ship this big? And fancy too. Wenches everywhere. No wenches on me pirate ship. Wonder where they keep the rum? Gotta find th' bridge—can almost feel th' wheel in me hands."

Jack turned his back on the security guard and spoke through clenched teeth. "Settle down. I can't carry on a conversation with you—people will think I'm talking to myself. And when Marcy shows up, I have to give my full attention to her. Can't have you yakking in my ear."

"I'll be quiet as a thief." Alejandro made a cross sign over his heart. "Pirate's honor."

"You gotta be kidding. Pirates have no…"

"Good morning—you must be Jack. I'm Marcy."

Jack spun around and extended his hand in introduction. "Thanks so much for your time and willingness to give me a tour. Our company is looking for a new venue for the annual sales meeting."

"I hope the *Island Princess* exceeds your expectations." Marcy smiled, distinct dimples appearing on her lightly freckled face. "She's the newest ship in our fleet. The latest and greatest of everything. Let's go to the pool area first—a favorite spot on a Caribbean cruise."

She chatted about the features of the ship as they strolled along the deck's length. The tailored white and navy blue-trimmed uniform complemented her slim figure. Francine had a long way to go before attaining her boss's shipshape appearance.

Although grateful, Jack was aware of Alejandro's conspicuous silence. He'd braced himself for the pirate's lewd comments about Marcy. When none came, he congratulated himself on finally subduing the ghost. But now, he couldn't even sense his ethereal presence, which was unusual. *Like a little kid—you worry when they're too quiet.*

Freakishly coincidental, the ship's mighty horn gave a series of short blasts followed by one long blast. Marcy stopped her spiel of information and frowned. She glanced at Jack. "How bizarre…" Her cell phone chirped. She tapped the screen and her eyes widened. "I'm so sorry—excuse me, Jack. I have to report to the bridge ASAP."

"Something must be wrong? The ship's horn sounded alarming."

"Yes. Seven short blasts followed by a long one means to abandon ship, which makes no sense since we're docked. Maybe it's some other emergency."

Pausing as if afraid of having said too much, she plastered a smile on her face and pointed to a set of large double doors. "Through there is the outdoor pool and bar. Please, order a drink, put it on my tab, and have a look around. I suspect this is all some mistake; I'll return shortly."

Jack pushed through the doors and spotted the bar, decorated with a grass roof and surrounded with flowering tropical plants. A beach ball that looked like a watermelon bounced back and forth between two teams splashing around in the pool. The players' shrieks and laughter filled the air. He smiled. *Spring breakers on vacation.*

Clusters of people surrounded the bar. Jack spotted the only unoccupied bar stool, partially obscured by a towering plant, its white flowers shaped like butterflies. He moved the wicker chair away from the clutches of the plant and settled in.

– 16 –

The Cruise Ship Tour

The high-energy scene pulled Jack in, brightening his mood. Piped-in calypso music maintained a steady beat. Jack observed the bartenders. They quickstepped around buzzing blenders and clattering ice machines with the grace of dancers, never missing a beat as they churned out enticing cocktails of every conceivable color. Coconut and pineapple wedges, spiral lemon peels and mint leaves adorned the many varieties of intoxicating beverages. Waiters delivered these works of art to sunbathers resting on pool loungers, who resembled glistening rotisserie chickens, turning every so often to evenly brown their skin.

With still no sign of the ghost, Jack muttered, "Alejandro. Where are you?"

No response. A cloak of dread swamped him. No doubt now. The fiendish pirate had discovered and infiltrated the command center of the ship.

Jack decided he needed an attitude check, and shrugged. *Why should I stress? Nobody can see Alejandro but me, so what's the worry? His pranks'll go unexplained.*

One of the bartenders, 'Nate from England' (according to the name-tag on his tropical floral shirt), approached Jack. "What'll it be?"

"Rum and coke with lime. Forget the umbrella."

Nate chuckled, plunging a scoop into a vat of ice. "Tired of foo-foo drinks, are ya?"

"Just trying to keep it simple. Marcy, the cruise director, told me to put this drink on her tab."

"Okay." He raised his eyebrows. "Marcy's feeling generous today." He finished Jack's drink with a lime slice and placed it before him.

"She's giving me a tour of the ship. I'm scouting out venues for a business trip."

Nate spun around and filled a plastic cup from a bulky machine fitted with an augur stirring a slushy pink cocktail. "Explains why you're the only one on that side of the bar not wearing a bathing suit." He garnished the drink with a bright blue umbrella and wedge of pineapple, set it on the bar, and gestured to someone behind Jack.

"I'm waiting for Marcy to return. She was called to the bridge."

"Here at the Tiki Bar, it's a steady stream of mostly naked bodies all day long." Nate grinned and picked up a vodka bottle in one hand, a martini shaker in the other, and executed the flip-and-pour trick. The bottle turned end-over-end; as Nate caught it the vodka was already flowing into the shaker.

A redhead wearing a navy blue polka dot string bikini bounced up to the bar. "I heard that. You're not complaining, are ya, Nate?" She picked up the fancy pink drink and scampered back to her friends.

Nate smiled and cocked an eyebrow. "Gotta love the spring breakers."

Jack grinned. "Tough job you've got." He gestured toward the pool. "I'm curious, did anybody react to those blasts from the ship's horn a few minutes ago?"

As if on cue, the calypso music ceased. The ship's public announcement system chimed three times, indicating a message to follow. A deep voice with an Italian accent filled the air:

"Good afternoon. This is your captain, Armando Schettino. Please disregard the warning sounds from the ship's horn. There is no emergency. A mechanical malfunction was found and corrected. We apologize for any inconvenience."

The music resumed. Jack smirked. *Yeah, right. A mechanical malfunction. More like a phantom menace.*

Nate leaned toward Jack and said, "In answer to your question—not much reaction from the partiers in the pool. Can't understand how a ship's horn could malfunction to make the specific signal for 'abandon ship.' Very strange." He shook his head and frowned.

A prolonged electronic screech blared from a nearby speaker, making Jack wince. And then, like a stink bomb, Alejandro's gravelly voice permeated the ship, belting out a bawdy limerick:

"I met me a wench in Barbados
'Er cart full of rum and potatoes,
She gave me a drink
And a lewd lil' wink,
Then fuckled me 'til th' next day-o.
Said life would be grand by 'er side,
So she forced me to make 'er me bride,
No dinner, no dance,
Just 'er hands in me pants
She diddled me 'til the low tide.

"Aaarr! Come and meet a real pirate on th' pool deck. Free rum punch for all me swashbucklin' mateys!"

The public address system cut off. Alejandro's raucous laughter hung on the air.

What the hell is that idiot doing? Jack shook his head. He glanced around, observing people's reaction. Most were laughing and scrambling out of the pool or from their chaise loungers, their excited chatter punctuated with the phrase 'free drinks.'

A woman behind him asked, "Did he say 'fuckled?' Can't believe the cruise line allows that kind of talk over their loudspeakers."

Another responded, "I didn't even know 'fuckled' was a word."

The two blathered on, their voices fading as they drifted away.

Jack smiled. *Gotta hand it to him. As pranks go, it's epic.* He watched as the line quickly formed for the free drinks. *Before this tour's over, things are gonna get real interesting.*

Nate and the other bartenders frowned and glanced around, as if expecting some explanation for the surprise rum punch giveaway. Finally Nate shrugged, raised his arms with hands palms-up, and called out, "I heard the same announcement you did. Must be an unscheduled promotion." Turning to his fellows, he said, "Better make some more of that punch. Something tells me we'll be runnin' through it." He then lined up ice-filled cups at the bar's edge and began pouring the rum concoction from a pitcher. He smiled and raised one of the glasses in a toast. "Bottoms up!"

The punch disappeared as fast as the bartenders could pour. People were pressing the bar, so Jack grabbed a free drink and left the crowded area. *Why shouldn't I take one? I deserve it—cartin' that ghost around.* He wove his way through the throng until he spotted a lounge chair shaded by a large potted palm tree by the pool. *Perfect.* Random thoughts tripped through his head. *How do they plant a mature tree into a pot? I wonder how much longer Marcy will be?*

He eased himself onto the cushioned recliner and wondered what the conversation might be like on the bridge. Two unexplained events. No evidence. *Ghosting has its advantages. Alejandro'd better be having the time of his life.* He laughed out loud at the irony. *Dead for three centuries, and having the time of his life. Why not?*

As Jack took the first sip of the rum punch, his nostrils flared at the familiar aroma of pipe smoke. In the bright light, he could barely detect Alejandro's pirate-y image.

"There you are," said Jack. "Been causin' trouble, ya knock-kneed bird-brain?"

"Yer startin' to talk like me. Knew I'd grow on ya." Alejandro floated to the chair next to Jack's and sat down. He rested his elbows on his knees, heaving an exaggerated sigh.

"What's the matter with you?" Jack smirked. "You got your wish. You're on the big ship. And now you're acting, what… grumpy?"

"This ol' salt wants to feel th' power o' the ocean tossin' th' ship, with th' wheel in me hands. Never seen a ship like this b'fore. No fuckin' wheel."

"You mean a helm's wheel?"

The ghost narrowed his eyes.

"You're acting like a spoiled brat," said Jack.

"How do ya run a ship wit' no wheel?"

"You obviously found the bridge."

"Just a bunch o' machines, all lit up an' blinkin'. Can't steer it."

"Let me cheer you up—let's see, we've been on the ship about a half hour and…" Jack ticked off the pirate's transgressions on his fingers. "You've tugged up a woman's skirt, blasted the horn to indicate 'abandon ship,' sung a filthy song, given away free rum punch, and now people expect to meet a…" He made air quotes with his fingers, "'real live pirate.' What's not to love?"

"Ya insensitive blighter. Gots to have a ship wit' a wheel."

"Can't help ya with that."

The ghost got up from the lounger. "Gonna drown me sorrows wit' a tankard o' rum, and th' love of a good woman.

Where's 'at sturdy wench, Francine? Bet she can take a good poundin'..."

"Knock it off. Leave Francine alone. Besides, you don't even have a real dick."

"Ye don't know nothin' about me Jolly Roger, ya ignorant toad. Remember me extry powers granted from up there," he pointed to the sky, "just for me last few days."

"And that's how you want to use your 'extry powers?' Awfully considerate of God, the Afterlife, or whatever, giving you the chance to get laid one last time." Jack put his head back and closed his eyes, hoping to discourage further conversation with the crabby ghost. The cacophony of approaching giggling and squealing young women caught his attention. One called out, "Last one in the pool's a rotten egg!"

Another replied, "That's so high school, Melanie. Go ahead. I'm heading for the free rum punch."

"Oh no, you're not. You're coming with me."

The women hit the pool, causing a low-grade tsunami and splashing Jack. He peeked out of one eye. Alejandro waggled his eyebrows, turning toward the pool. "Aaarrr! Me favorite—drunk wenches in th' water! Jump in, Jack. We'll have 'em mewin' like a basket of kittens 'fore we're done wit' 'em."

"Maybe I will. I'm hot, and now my clothes are wet."

With no response from the ghost, Jack assumed he'd drifted toward the rowdy girls in the pool. He opened both eyes and focused his attention on the antics, holding his breath, anticipating another prank from Alejandro. Suddenly, the scene before him down-shifted to a crawl. The happy sounds from the pool became tinny and distant. In spite of the hot day, his sweat turned icicle-cold, and he felt lightheaded.

"What the fuck..." He blinked. Finally, his brain caught up to what his eyes had already registered. *Rachel! What the hell is she doing here?*

– 17 –

Cruise Ship Tour, Part 2

Jack could think of nothing worse than facing Rachel, especially with an out-of-control ghost on the loose. He willed himself to be invisible and tried to slink unobtrusively from the lounger, but the buckle on his sandal caught in the loose weave of the cushion. He jerked his leg to free his foot, but the lounger tipped over, giving his ankle a mighty twist. In pain and off-balance, his flailing arm caught the plastic cup of rum punch and sent it flying as he toppled onto the unforgiving concrete.

He prayed the commotion of the metal chair clattering against the deck wouldn't draw Rachel's attention. It'd be epically humiliating if she witnessed his clumsiness. Lying full length on the concrete, Jack wiggled his foot free and left the sandal stuck in the cushion.

"Sir, let me help you up." Jack glanced up and saw the concerned face of a white-uniformed crew member. He extended his hand to Jack.

"That's okay. I'm fine." Jack scrambled to his feet, careful to avoid the red puddle of rum punch. He ran his hand through his hair, trying to appear blasé.

"Is your ankle hurt?" The man frowned and glanced down at Jack's bare foot.

"No. My shoe just got stuck in the cushion." He offered a bland smile. "That's all."

The crewman disentangled the sandal and handed it to him. "Thanks," said Jack, with a nod. At least the man was blocking him from the view of the people in the pool.

He darted behind the potted palm, clutched his wrenched ankle, and swore under his breath. "Shit. Shit. Shit." *I hope I didn't break my frickin' ankle. Damn it! If it weren't for that ghost, and now Rachel...* "Great, just great."

He peered around the tree's trunk and studied the women in the pool. They seemed oblivious to the ruckus he'd caused. Rachel and her friends were shrieking and laughing in the water, sitting on each other's shoulders, playing Chicken Fight.

Yeah, that's it—laugh it up, Rachel. Don't let a little matter like pulling the plug on our wedding stand in the way of your fun.

Jack counted eight women and recognized about half. The memory of a long-ago conversation with Rachel surfaced: *"My friend Melanie invited me to her bachelorette party. It's on a Caribbean cruise—in February. Ha, won't you be jealous."*

He muttered, "So this is the bachelorette party. Of all the damned cruise ships in the Caribbean—why did it have to be this one?"

And why am I hiding like a skulking Peeping Tom? Disgusted with himself, Jack frowned and cast a disparaging glance at the enormous plant providing his cover. Favoring his hurt ankle, he leaned against the trunk of the tree for support. He put the sandal back on, loosening the strap to accommodate his already-swelling ankle.

Watching Rachel frolic in the pool unlocked the inner gate that kept his frustrating memories corralled. *Never bothered to answer my calls, my emails. Not a scrap of closure.* He shook his head in disgust. *Why put everyone through the drama of a canceled wedding? You couldn't even tell me yourself. What a coward.*

He recalled the anguished look on Amy's face, Rachel's maid of honor, when she delivered the bad news that his bride had taken off. It'd been particularly upsetting because Amy, his friend since childhood, had introduced them. She and Rachel had been sorority sisters and best friends. After the wedding debacle, the women's friendship ended.

Emboldened, he lurched toward the pool's edge, ready to confront Rachel, taking a perverse pleasure in the element of surprise. He pictured the smile on her face dissolving like cotton candy in the hot sun when she saw him. But then he thought of Jessica and stopped. *Why waste any time or energy on the past?* He spun around, wincing at the jolt of pain the movement caused his ankle, and limped away from the pool. Putting Rachel behind him, literally and figuratively, felt like a win.

Jack hobbled over to the other side of the ship, as far away from the pool as he could get. He leaned on the ship's railing and rested his injured foot on the bottom rung. The turquoise surface of the Caribbean rippled from a steady breeze. A couple of jet skis, sounding like a million buzzing wasps, whizzed by. The sun felt good on his face, like a vitamin D rush. He closed his eyes and thought of Jessica. He wanted to be with her, and be done with Alejandro, the cruise ship, and Rachel.

Jack glanced down and noticed that several decks below, some passengers were boarding one of the ship's bright orange tenders, a small vessel that functioned as both lifeboat and water taxi. Based on their gear, the cruisers were going snorkeling. The tender left the cruise ship and headed out to sea toward another boat that had Blue Tang Diving and Snorkeling stenciled on its starboard side. *Maybe a cruise vacation would be fun. Adventurous side trips, great food, drinks, entertainment.* He pictured himself on a cruise with Jessica, visiting countries like Spain, France, and Italy. Judging from her enthusiasm for the meal he'd cooked last night, she appreciated good food and wine. He knew she'd love the cuisine of the Mediterranean region.

He sensed a presence behind him, interrupting his daydreaming, and turned, expecting to see Marcy ready to resume their tour. Instead, Rachel came into view, wearing a barely there animal-print bikini top and a sarong tied at her waist. Jack froze. His heart beat strong enough to rattle his rib cage.

Whoa. His eyes widened, and he gawked at Rachel's chest. *What the fuck... unbelievable. She got a boob job.* The bolt-on boobs looked like they came from a catalog. Perfectly round, no jiggle, no bounce.

Her vacation tan couldn't hide the red creeping up from her neck to her forehead, revealing her embarrassment. "I thought that was you by the pool. Wow. What are the chances we'd be on the same cruise?" Rachel glanced down at her feet. "Are you here on a business trip? Or are you trying to catch up to me?" She squinched her eyes, using her hand as a shield from the intense sun as she gazed up at him.

He relished her fidgeting discomfort. "Huh. Don't flatter yourself, Rachel. I'm *not* following you to the ends of the earth." He turned away from her to gaze out at the ocean. "I see you're re-entering the dating scene with enhanced gear. What'd you do, Rachel, race to the plastic surgeon's office directly from the church?"

"No." She sighed. "Look, I don't know where to begin, Jack."

"How about, 'I'm so sorry I fucked you over on our wedding day?'" He refused to look her way, preferring to let her talk to his cold shoulder.

"I was overwhelmed—just couldn't commit to a lifetime..."

"A lifetime with good ol' boring Jack? A nice guy, but really not all that exciting?"

"I know I hurt you...but I felt trapped," said Rachel. "Scared."

"Really? Scared? Scared of what...me, or life? You broke my heart. You completely shut me out, and then ignored all my attempts to contact you. I deserved some kind of closure, but you were, what...too...stingy to throw even a scrap of explanation my way?"

"Look at me, Jack, please."

"I have nothing to say to you, Rachel, and right now, I really don't want to hear anything you have to say either."

"Please, don't be like that." She waited, leaving an opening for Jack to respond. He was silent. "Okay...I get it. You're angry. For what it's worth, I planned on calling you when I got back from this bachelorette party. But, I guess fate is throwing us together now, so I'll just say it. Jack, I made a huge mistake, and...I still love you."

Selfish, stingy and silent, and now this? He stared at the ocean and shook his head in disbelief. A breeze ruffled Jack's hair, carrying with it the faint aroma of pipe smoke. "Rachel, it's over between us."

"But, Jack—"

"Drop it. You don't stand a ghost of a chance."

She frowned, opened her mouth as if to say something, then turned and walked away, quickly fading from his peripheral vision. He took a deep breath, realizing he'd barely been breathing. *Un-be-fucking-lievable. Nothing from her in months, and then a face-to-face on my so-called get-away from all her bullshit.*

Jack's throbbing, barking ankle claimed his attention. He sat down in the nearest chair, now wondering if the ankle was fractured instead of sprained. He loosened the sandal's strap again just as he noticed Marcy approaching. *Finally. Let's finish this damned tour and get me the hell out of here.*

Marcy seemed stressed and a little short of breath. "Sorry

I was gone so long—and then it took me awhile to find you. I thought you'd be hanging out at the bar."

"I had a couple of drinks," said Jack, "including a free rum punch. I moved over here for the ocean view."

"Crazy afternoon. Lots of strange activity," said Marcy.

"The announcement of free rum punch sure lured the crowds. Do you often run free drink promotions on this cruise ship?" Jack smiled. His ankle and Rachel had put him in a prickly mood, so he took a perverse enjoyment in stirring the pot, smug in the knowledge that only he understood what was behind all the commotion.

"No. We *never* offer free drinks. Ever." A frustrated expression strained her face. "Somehow someone infiltrated our public address system and pulled that prank. The Captain's furious. As of a few minutes ago, the free rum punch stopped flowing."

"How about the ship's horn blasting? What was that all about?"

Jack stood up and gingerly put weight on his foot. He gimped along, following Marcy as she moved further away from the noisy crowd. "Can't explain the horn. None of it makes any sense. We have strict security on this ship, and only the navigation officers were on the bridge."

"Maybe a ghost slipped on board."

"At this point, I'd believe anything. Because of all the bizarre events this afternoon, I have to attend a meeting in a half hour. Francine is available to finish up your tour." She glanced down at his foot and frowned. "Are you limping?"

"A little. Turned my ankle—the buckle on my sandal got caught in the cushion of a lounge chair."

"I'm sorry to hear that—looks kind of puffy. We can end the tour if walking bothers you."

"Probably a good idea. I should ice and elevate it." He glanced at his watch. An hour had passed. "I've taken up enough of your time."

"You haven't taken up my time; the mystery prankster has. I have a few minutes before my meeting. Would you like to wrap it up with a quick look at one of our staterooms? The mini-suites are very nice, and include a balcony."

"Sure." Jack winced and limped along. *The last thing I wanna do.*

A whiff of pipe smoke wafted under his nose, putting him on high alert. Alejandro's raspy whisper filled his ear. "Ask 'er where 'at wench, Francine, went."

Jack made a go-away gesture. The aroma dissipated. *I wonder what would happen if I left his undead ass on the ship?*

"We're going to the Dolphin Deck—that's the ninth deck, five below this one. There's one unoccupied mini-suite I can show you." Marcy fixed her gaze on Jack. "Most businesses pick the suites for their employees."

He nodded and smiled at her upsell tactics. *Of course, the suites cost more than the interior cabins.* "Thanks. Good to know." *Poor woman. I feel like a jerk leading her on about a business trip. All for a pain-in-the-ass ghost.*

They stepped into an elevator and inched their way down. Glistening cruisers crowded in at every stop, the small space quickly flooding with the scent of sunscreen and lotions. Finally, the doors opened on the Dolphin Deck. Jack limped out of the confined space, feeling grateful nobody had tromped on his injured ankle.

Jack smiled at Marcy. "The smells of vacation—suntan lotion and rum."

She shot him a rueful look. "Follow me. The suite is down the hall a little way."

Marcy paused in front of a door and glanced at her cell phone. "According to my notes, this is it—room 926." She fished a key from her pocket and inserted it into the lock, but hesitated before turning the knob. "Did you hear that?" She glanced at Jack, her eyebrows furrowing.

"Hear what?"

"Sounds like somebody's in there. According to the steward's log, this room's been vacant all week."

Jack moved closer to the door. He detected the distinct moans and gasps of hanky-panky. "Um, I think you're right. This room is most definitely occupied."

Marcy shook her head and opened her mouth as if to comment. A prolonged squeal, followed by giggling and a loud thump against the door, made them both step back.

Francine's muffled-yet-unmistakable voice cried out, "Alejandro, ya naughty pirate! Plunder me honeypot, or ye'll walk the plank..."

"Okay," Marcy said, "Enough of that. Time to move on." She hurried away in the direction of the elevator.

Jack pressed his lips together, holding in his laughter. *How the hell does he do it?* "I guess today isn't the best day for a tour, is it?"

"Perhaps not." She sighed and shook her head. "I'm sorry, Jack. In spite of all the, uh, peculiar events today, I hope you'll consider us for your business event."

"Sure thing. I'll tell my boss there's never a dull moment on your ship."

They reached the elevator. "Call me with any questions, Jack. I'd love to see you next year with your sales team." Marcy smiled—Jack thought it looked stretched—and shook his hand. "You can disembark on the third deck, the same place you came on board. Enjoy the rest of your day, and say hello to Jessica for me."

"Will do. Since I didn't get a chance to, er, see Francine again, please thank her for me."

She cocked one eyebrow. "Rest assured, I'll be speaking to Francine very soon."

Jack stepped into the crowded elevator and slumped against the wall, eyes closed, grateful to be done with the charade. *Great. Now Francine's in trouble. I'm outta here, with or without Alejandro.* After stopping at every level on the way down, the doors finally opened to the third deck, and the remaining people, mostly senior citizens, spilled out into the already-packed disembarkation area. A crewman held up a sign that read: Tortuga Rum Cake Factory Tour. The crowd funneled onto the metal gangway. Jack glanced out the window and saw a couple of buses idling at the ready. The rum cake excursion obviously catered to the geriatric set. Walkers, canes, and thick-soled comfy shoes were well-represented. *From bikinis to blue-hairs. This cruise has it all.*

Jack scanned the crowd, looking for Alejandro. After listening to the ghost and Francine going at it like teenagers, Jack thought the pirate might choose to stay on the ship. *Wishful thinking.*

As the last person ambled down the gangway, Jack wondered how long he could loiter in the area before a crewmember asked him what he was up to. *I'll give that frickin' ghost five more minutes, then I'm gone.* He tried to be inconspicuous, peering out a window facing the ocean. A tender bobbed in the water, close to the ship. Two crewmen worked from the small boat using long-handled paint rollers, touching up the royal blue stripe on the ship's otherwise-gleaming white hull.

"Excuse me, sir."

Jack turned around to face a man dressed in a crisp white uniform, the word "Security" stenciled in yellow on his navy blue vest.

"May I help you?" asked the square-jawed man. "Are you looking for someone?" Although polite, he projected a no-nonsense vibe. Security gadgets clipped to various places on his clothing gave Jack the impression he could summon a posse in a matter of seconds.

"Um, not exactly," answered Jack. "In fact, I'm leaving the ship. Came on board for a tour."

"Ah, I see," the man smiled. "This is a secure area, so..."

"Of course. I'll go now." He gestured to the window. "Just

watching the painters. Must be constant maintenance on a ship this size."

"Yes, there's always work to be done, sir."

"Okay, then. Have a good day," said Jack. He hurried as fast as he could to the gangway ramp. *Frickin' tardy ghost. I guess you're on your own now, pal.*

Alejandro superimposed himself onto Jack just as he set foot on the gangway ramp. The surprise and impact of the extra weight were a direct hit on his sore ankle. Jack stumbled and clutched the railing for stability, muttering, "A warning would've been nice, asshole."

"Thought ya was made of sturdier stuff, ya lame mongrel."

"Nice. Thanks for the insult, you ungrateful..."

"Padlock yer gob, matey. Got me one more thing to do before headin' back to land."

Alejandro's weight abruptly lifted. Jack frowned and straightened. *Where the hell did he go?*

Jack turned his head just in time to see Alejandro's filmy image leaping onto the tender with the painters, now just a couple feet from the concrete pier. The ghost's weight connected with one of the paint buckets and sent it flying, flinging the blue color against the white hull. The two workers scrambled to keep the other bucket upright.

Jack's mouth fell open as he watched the slapstick scene play out. Through the bright sunshine he could barely make out Alejandro, who'd commandeered one of the long-handled paint rollers, using it to push both workers into the ocean.

The pirate shouted, "Kiss me hairy arse, Blackbeard! Ya ain't never had a vessel like this one." Jack watched as the tender's wheel spun wildly back and forth before the boat took off like a shot, narrowly missing the concrete pier on one side and the cruise ship on the other. He could hear Alejandro's lusty laughter over the dull roar of the boat's engine, quickly fading into the distance.

– 18 –

Afternoon Delight

The *tink* of glass against glass penetrated Jack's drowsy state. Semi-reclined and too lazy to open both eyes, he peeked from the right one. Jessica rocked a pearl-white bikini studded with tiny turquoise beads—a striking contrast to her Caribbean skin tone. She placed two frosted, longneck beers garnished with lime slices on the small poolside table.

Jessica leaned over Jack. A delicate coconut scent mingled with the aroma of her skin, warm from the sun. She kissed him and whispered, "How's my patient? Ready for a beer?"

"Definitely. You spoil me." Jack wiggled his foot, now wrapped in an ice pack and elevated on a pile of beach towels.

Jessica settled into the lounger next to Jack's. She held up her beer bottle. "Cheers." She gestured toward his foot. "Other than a twisted ankle, tell me what else happened today."

"Where do I begin?" Jack squeezed the lime into the beer bottle. "For starters, before we even got on the ship, Alejandro announced he wanted to get laid."

"What?" Jessica raised an eyebrow.

"Yup. It all went downhill from there."

"I'm all ears."

Jack entertained Jessica with the ghost's antics, ending with he and Marcy over-hearing Alejandro and Francine's sexual romp in a guest suite.

"How does he do it?" asked Jessica. "I mean, is his penis… real?"

"Well, I asked him and he told me I didn't 'know nothin' about his Jolly Roger.' And then he called me an 'ignorant toad.' He reminded me he was gifted with extra powers, whatever that means, for his last few days as a ghost."

"His extra powers must've included sex."

"Imagine me telling this story to anyone else." Jack shook his head. "They'd think I was a lunatic."

"If I hadn't experienced Alejandro, I'd think you were nuts."

"See what I mean?"

"He's more alive than dead… an amped-up ghost, like a poltergeist, causing disturbances and moving stuff." Jessica frowned. "Did Alejandro leave with you? Or is he still on the ship, serving out his last days as Francine's love-ghost?"

"I saved the best for last." Jack grinned. "He hijacked one of the ship's tenders."

"What?" Jessica sat up in the lounge chair.

"Yeah. Wish you could've seen that. Earlier, he'd complained the 'big ship' didn't have a wheel, so he couldn't take it out to sea. As we were leaving, he jumped onto a maintenance tender carrying two painters and buckets of blue paint."

"And—he actually took off with the boat?"

"He sure did. But not before flinging blue paint all over the hull of the ship, then pushing both men in the drink."

"Oh no. That goes way above-and-beyond mere ghostly mischief…. Were the men okay?"

"Yeah. They wore life jackets, but imagine how shocked they were. Pushed into the ocean by unseen hands."

"Alejandro sounds like he's getting dangerous."

"I think he was so hell-bent on steering a boat again, nothing was going to stop him."

"Could you see him?"

"Yeah, in spite of the bright sun. He spun the wheel back

and forth, cursed Blackbeard, and then took off. The security guy watched the whole thing, along with a few other crewmen. I heard their comments. They thought the tender had malfunctioned, and sent another boat after it."

"How far did Alejandro get?" asked Jessica.

"According to one of the crewmen, the tender crashed into a fish market on the beach in Georgetown."

"I sure hope nobody was hurt."

Jack grimaced. "I grabbed a cab and told the driver to cruise by the fish market. It must've been just a little shack. Nothing left but a pile of lumber, and fish strewn all over the sand. Nobody seemed to be injured."

Jessica matched his expression. "Where is Alejandro now?" she asked.

"Who knows? He definitely ended up on land, because the tender was smashed up on the beach."

"Do you think we'll ever see him again? He sure has a lot to answer for."

"Time will tell." Jack moved his foot and winced.

"Enough of that whacked-out ghost. Time to check my patient." Jessica got up from her lounger and felt the ice pack. "Could use some fresh ice. How's it feel?"

"Ankle's not so good, but other parts of me are excellent, thanks to your bikini. Wanna see?"

Jack hooked his arm around Jessica's waist and pulled her onto his lap. She scrunched her eyebrows together in a mock stern look. "As your personal physician, I can't condone any activity that might cause further injury to your ankle."

"I'm a tough guy—I can deal with the pain."

"Seriously? The way you were whining when you got back from the ship—or was that just a sympathy ploy?"

"Maybe." He slipped his hand into the back of her bikini bottom and squeezed. "You think my ankle's swollen, you oughta see my..."

She batted his hand away. "You're as bad as Alejandro."

He cupped her chin and kissed her—a lingering, soft kiss. A lock of hair fell onto her forehead, and he tucked it back in place.

Jessica pulled her pink-framed sunglasses down her nose and stared into Jack's eyes. She traced a circle around his nipple with her index finger. A flirtatious smile danced around her mouth. "Maybe we should go up to my condo. An injury such as yours requires bed rest."

"Hmmm... a healer *and* a mind reader. My lucky day."

A little while later, Jack lazed in a tangle of sheets on Jessica's bed. He stretched and turned over on his back. Carrots, Jessica's orange tabby cat, apparently viewed this movement as an invitation and deftly leapt up on the bed. He began kneading the pillow, his purr motor running full throttle. Jack reached out to pet him. The cat pressed his head into Jack's hand, and the purring cranked up a few more decibels.

Jack continued to pet the contented cat, mulling over his crazy day with the pirate. *And then there was Rachel.* He'd left out that tidbit when recapping his day to Jessica. *I'll tell her about it—when the time is right.*

He stared at the ceiling fan's rotating blades. The motion lulled him into a reflective state as he pondered the aspects of his new situation. *I'm in love. I'm happy. Gotta change my life.* He flinched at the strange thought. *The careful planning, the successful career. Change that? For the unknown? For love?*

Jessica's voice interrupted the questions streaming through his head. "Hey, there." She walked from the bathroom and perched on the edge of the bed. Her accompanying floral-scented cloud and damp hair indicated she'd had a recent shower. She took Jack's hand, the one that'd been petting the cat, and kissed it. "Bonding with Carrots?"

"I think he likes me. He purrs a lot. Is that a good sign?"

"Definitely. You get the paw of approval."

Carrots hopped off the bed, flattening his ears—a sign he was irritated with the interruption of his petting session. He sauntered out of the room, tail in the air.

Jessica shook her head and laughed. "Cat attitudes." She leaned into Jack for a kiss. "By any chance, you hungry?"

"You bet I'm hungry." He smiled at her and caressed her cheek with his thumb. "Rum punch doesn't stick to your ribs. And then you plied me with frosty beers, which turned out to be just a scheme to have your way with me."

"Oh, is that how it was? Last I remember, you were blaming my bikini." She tossed him a sideways glance, mischief flickering in her eyes.

He tapped the end of her nose with his finger. "No matter how you spin it, I think you're a schemer." Jack propped himself up on the pillow. "But a charming schemer." He shifted his gaze to her aqua-blue sundress. "You look stunning. How 'bout going out for dinner?"

"You must've read my mind. May I suggest the Calypso Grill? It's one of my faves. Picture this: a romantic candlelit table by the ocean, a bottle of wine, and delicious food."

"I'm in. Easy to sell this starving man."

"Normally we'd need reservations, but it's a bit early, so perhaps they can seat us. We'll be back here in time for 'Alejandro hour.'"

"That's right. You hope to hear from your favorite pirate tonight. Think he'll keep his promise to you?"

"Hope so. He knows I want to hear about my ancestors. After all, he's the one who made a big deal about going on the cruise ship tour in exchange for the stories."

"Yeah. Well, remember he's a ghost—and not particularly a man of his word." He patted her knee. "Don't be disappointed if he doesn't show. For all we know, he's already crossed over."

Jessica sighed. "If it's meant to be, then we'll see him. Otherwise..."

"In spite of him being an enormous pain in the ass, he did, in a way, bring us together. I'll be forever grateful for that."

"Same here." She stood, offering her hands. "Tick tock. Shower time. It's lobster season, and you're the only thing standing between me and dinner."

Jack grabbed her hands and sprung to his feet, wincing from the weight on his sore ankle.

Jessica glanced down. "Any improvement?"

"Better than it was, thanks to your nursing skills. Think of it—this is the second time you've tended to me in only three days."

"I know. Starting with your swollen hand from punching that guy on the beach." She furrowed her brow. "I wonder how his nose is doing?"

"Well, I wouldn't want to trade places with him. I'd rather have a sprained ankle than my nose pointing in the wrong direction."

Palm trees lined the stone path leading up to the entrance of the Calypso Grill, their trunks wrapped in twinkling blue lights. An oversized chalkboard menu sat propped up against an indigo-colored ceramic pot, home to a spiky yucca plant.

"Look!" Jessica squeezed Jack's arm and pointed at the menu. "I'm in heaven—six different kinds of lobster dishes."

He grinned and put his arm around her waist, enjoying her enthusiasm for food. He pictured them cooking together someday.

Jack spoke with the hostess, and soon they were seated at an outdoor table with a view of Morgan's Harbor. Boats tied up to the wooden docks bobbed in the rippling water. The setting was perfect for the conversation he wanted to have.

Moments later, a waiter approached the table with an iced champagne bucket and two flutes. He presented the bottle of Taittinger champagne to Jack, who nodded his approval.

Jessica threw Jack a surprised look. "We didn't even order yet. Is this guy a mind reader?"

"Called ahead and set it up." Jack leaned in toward Jessica. "Told them it was an exceptional night, and I wanted to make a good impression on a beautiful woman."

"I could get used to this, Jack." She lowered her head and fixed her gaze on him. "I mean, what *is* this *thing* between us?"

The waiter filled their flutes with bubbly and slipped away.

Jack raised his glass. "To this wonderful 'thing' between us, that I'm convinced is love."

Jessica touched her glass to his and nodded, smiling. She sipped the champagne. "Excellent choice. You know how to spoil a girl."

"You're uneasy about me saying that I love you, aren't you?"

She glanced away and fixed her gaze on the ocean. "We've only known each other a few days, so I wonder, how can we be in love?"

"I feel like we're living, or at least I'm living, the charming cliché of 'love at first sight.'"

"Maybe it's possible." She returned her gaze to his face. "I'm very attracted to you, and have strong feelings for you. I remind myself that you're recovering from a broken relationship—and on vacation in a very romantic setting." She shrugged. "So, is it love or infatuation?"

"After seeing Rachel on the ship today, I know I'm truly in love with you. There's no comparison."

Her jaw dropped. "You saw your ex-fiancée on the ship today?"

"Yes. I was saving that part of the story 'til now."

"Let me get this straight. You told me all about Alejandro's tricks and pranks, but you left out the juicy nugget about Rachel being on the ship?" Jessica's eyes widened.

"I saw her in the cruise ship's pool with a bunch of her girlfriends. It took me a minute, but then I remembered some time ago she'd been invited to a bachelorette party on a Caribbean cruise ship." He smirked. "And some people say there's no such thing as a coincidence."

He focused on Jessica's face, anticipating her reaction. Her furrowed brow and pursed lips weren't encouraging.

While Jack considered his next move, a pelican appeared in his peripheral vision. Flying low and close by, the bird folded itself into a feathery missile and plunged into the water with a noisy splash.

Jessica startled. "Wow—that was close!"

He peered over the railing. "Look, Jessica—he got his dinner." They watched as a silvery fish disappeared with one gulp into the pelican's large, rubbery throat pouch.

Jack reached for his champagne glass. "Shall we toast to our feathered friend's catch of the day?"

"Did you cue up the water show to distract me from the subject of Rachel?"

"Pelicans will do anything for a fish dinner."

Jessica met Jack's gaze. "So, what'd you think when you saw her?"

"I wanted to confront her, but then I thought of you, and turned away."

"Did she see you?" asked Jessica.

Jack nodded. "After I limped my way across the ship to get away from her, she sort of crept up behind me a few minutes later."

"Wow. That's bold."

"She'd had a boob job." Jack rolled his eyes.

"And ... how'd you determine that?"

"She wore a bikini that barely covered them. Hell, a priest would've noticed."

"What'd she say to you?"

"She thought it was the appropriate time since, in her words, 'fate had thrown us together,' to tell me she'd make a huge mistake. That she still loves me."

"That's heavy." Jessica hesitated, furrowing her brows. "How do you feel about that?"

"I felt nothing but scorn for her. But, I did get the closure I was seeking."

"Do you miss her?" asked Jessica.

"Not one iota."

Jessica reached across the table and laid her hand on top of Jack's. "Good. Rachel's *persona non grata*. Let's enjoy our dinner for two."

– 19 –

Ricky Meets Jack

Sated with lobster, Jack and Jessica returned to the condo, kicked off their shoes, and headed to the beach. Holding hands, they strolled the water's edge. Lights from hotels and resorts spilled onto the seashore, dimly illuminating their path. Jack wondered about island living. *Pure paradise, or not?*

Jessica squeezed his hand. "What are you thinking?"

"What's it like to live on a small island in the Caribbean?"

"Most of the time, it's wonderful, but island fever can set in. A seventy-five square mile patch of land can feel confining, and even downright claustrophobic. That's why I occasionally need to get away."

Jessica's comment reminded him that his time on the island was running short. It'd be all he could do to leave her and drag himself to the airport.

"I only have two more nights with you, and then it's back to reality and snowy Michigan."

"Don't want to think about that right now." Jessica glanced up at him with a slight frown.

He paused and turned toward her, gathering her close. Tiny waves rippled and danced over their feet. Returning to his workaday world represented a colossal interference to nurturing their budding relationship. The fear of losing Jessica because of distance was a sobering possibility.

He kissed her and murmured, "I want you to miss me when I'm gone. I want you to think about me every waking moment, and then I want you to dream about me."

"Oh, Jack. I don't want you to leave." She wrapped her arms around his neck and pressed her body into his.

"I can't get enough of you, Jessica. You light me up inside and out."

"Where do we go from here?"

"Why don't you come to Michigan next month for a visit?" He rubbed her back, hoping to coax out the response he wanted to hear.

"I'd like nothing better." Jessica leaned back and locked gazes with him. She took a deep breath, letting it out as she said, "But March is our busiest month. I can't leave."

He forced what he hoped was an understanding smile, and then asked, "How about April?"

"April isn't good either." She shook her head. "The snow-birds maintain a steady stream from north to south throughout May."

Jack's smile faded. *Sounds like a total shut-out.*

Jessica raised her eyebrows. "You have a new customer here, plus the one in Miami. Maybe you'll have a reason to see them again in March or April and sneak down here for a few days?" She held up crossed fingers. "A girl can hope."

"I like how you think. I can probably arrange that."

Jessica smiled and grabbed his hand, resuming their leisurely stroll. "Let's go check the calendar. I already can't wait to see you again."

She's into me. Or, testing me to see how far I'll go out of my way for her? Ever hopeful, he considered the possibility that she was falling in love with him in turn.

"Hi, Jessica," said a male voice from behind them.

Jack spun around, surprised by the unwanted interruption. The ambient light revealed a short, well-built man standing a few feet away. He wore a pair of binoculars around his neck. His hands-on-hips stance radiated a threatening vibe.

He knows her name, and he looks pissed off. Jack instinctively moved to block the guy's access to Jessica. With his newly injured ankle and sore hand from the beach fight a couple nights ago, he had no desire for another physical confrontation.

The intruder made a show of slowly crossing his arms over his chest. "Long time no see, Jess. You're lookin' fine." He jerked his head in Jack's direction. "Who's your friend?" He emphasized the word "friend" nastily, smirking.

"Ricky. What are you doing here?" Jessica's tone was calm and quiet.

"What am *I* doing here? I live here. I'll ask again, who's your *friend*, Jessica?"

Jack stuck out his hand in introduction. "I'm Jack. That satisfy you?"

"Well, Jack, did you know Jessica's my wife?" Ricky unfolded his arms and bulldozed his hand into Jack's with a jaws-of-death grip, not letting go.

Jack winced. "You tryin' to prove something with your caveman handshake?" With his left hand he dealt a karate-chop blow to Ricky's arm, breaking the grip and freeing himself.

"Stop acting like a jackass, Ricky," said Jessica. "We've been divorced for over a year. I'm not your wife."

"Man's law, Jess, not God's law." He pointed up at the sky, as if God was on his side.

"Let it go, man," said Jack.

"Why don't you shut the fuck up? This is between Jessica and me."

"There's nothing between us," said Jessica.

Jack took Jessica's hand and said, "Let's get outta here." They started walking away, but Ricky grabbed Jack's arm.

"I'm not done with you, asshole."

Jack twisted his arm free. "Yeah, you are done. Jessica's not interested in hearing any more of your bullshit. Leave her alone, and move on with your life." *Gotta get away from this lunatic before he turns really violent.* "Come on, Jessica. We have an appointment with a ghost."

They left a speechless Ricky behind. When they reached the condo complex, Jack turned and looked back. "I think he's gone."

"Oh, Jack." Jessica sagged against him. "I'm so sorry about that. I thought he'd moved—left the island."

"No reason to apologize. It's not your fault he appeared out of nowhere." He hugged her, and they walked toward their building.

Jessica gestured to the wooden bench by the pool. "Let's sit here for a minute."

"Same bench from two nights ago, after the beach fight," said Jack, flashing a sardonic smile. "Been piling up injuries—nothin' but one adventure after another since I arrived."

Jessica scowled and picked up Jack's hand. "Did Ricky hurt your hand?"

"Well, he didn't improve it." He flexed his fingers. "It was still sore from the other night, and now it's worse."

"Where'd you learn that move you used on Ricky?"

"I took a self-defense class at MSU." Jack grinned. "Got an A."

"Impressive. It caught Ricky off-guard. The look on his face was pure surprise."

"Seems like it doesn't take much to set Ricky off. Is he going to be a problem for you?"

"I hope not." Jessica closed her eyes and sighed. "The last I heard he'd enrolled in Miami Dade's electrician program. Now he's back, which means he quit the program or flunked out. I sure didn't like being surprised by him."

"Kind of odd that he's walking around with binoculars at night," said Jack. "Wonder what he's up to?"

A frown creased Jessica's forehead. "Makes me feel like he's stalking me, or us. The whole thing's bizarre."

A thought poked Jack and took root. He stared up at the starry sky, mulling over his theory. "Maybe he knew we were here. Is he the sneaky type, the sort that'd plant a GPS locator somewhere on your car?"

"Umm... what makes you think that?"

"When you said the word 'stalking,' it reminded me of a guy I work with. He has a teenage daughter that's a real handful—always in trouble. He couldn't trust her. He put a tracker on her car so he could monitor her whereabouts. Told me he felt like one of those stalking parents."

Jessica whispered, "Oh my God. What if Ricky attached one of those things to my car? Can we find it?"

"Maybe. It's too dark now, but in the morning we'll check. If we don't see anything, let's take it to a mechanic for an inspection, just to be sure."

"Now you know why I'm cautious about new relationships. One Mr. Wrong in a lifetime is enough." Jessica tossed Jack a rueful smile. "Ricky can't seem to get it through his thick head that we're finished. Forever."

"I do wonder why you married him. Was he always such a jerk?"

"No. But I came to realize he was paranoid—always wanting to know who I worked with, who I talked to, where I was. He showed some of that behavior when we were teens, but I just thought it was proof of how much he loved me."

"Sometimes, it's hard to recognize the signs." Jack shrugged. "I missed clues about Rachel."

Jessica nodded. "I assumed Ricky felt unhappy working for someone else—he always defied authority, resisted taking direction. I thought he'd rather do his own thing, so we started a pool cleaning business. He was to manage and run it."

"What happened?" asked Jack.

"He barely worked... stole cash from the company. I

thought the responsibility of owning a business would be good for him—that he'd bounce back to his former, happier self."

"Can't accuse you of not trying to make the marriage work." Jack took her hand and squeezed it.

"In hindsight, I recognize the relationship was lopsided. Ricky became my project. I wanted to save him, help him, change him. Whatever. Pick one. Not a sound basis for a marriage."

"Sounds like he needs professional help."

"He does. I suggested it once. He lashed out and told me I should focus on being a better wife."

"Ricky's a dangerous stalker, Jessica."

"He's become an insane version of himself. Such a waste."

"I'm sorry he's back on the island." Jack squeezed her hand again.

Jessica's frown dissolved, and a little smile played around her mouth. "So, what was 'we have an appointment with a ghost' all about?"

"Hey, it's the truth. Ricky wanted a showdown, and I wanted to defuse the situation, so that's what popped out. Maybe he'll avoid you, thinking you're crazy and consorting with ghosts."

"Quick thinking. Lately, this beach seems to have developed an element of danger." Jessica paused and stared into the distance.

"What's up?" Jack nudged Jessica to snap her out of her stare.

"An aha moment just hit me. When we stopped at that little beach after the Mud Slide lunch ... do you suppose Ricky could've been the mysterious man who offered to pay those boys to hit us with the beach ball?"

"You think he tracked us to that beach?"

"Yes. If we buy into the assumption that he put some sort of device on my car, it adds up, doesn't it?"

"It does. Do you think he'd pull a prank like that?"

"Possible. Since he can't move on past the divorce, I guess he'll try to meddle in my relationships any way he can." Jessica heaved a huge sigh. "Let's go inside. I feel strange—like I'm exposed, or being watched."

"Sure thing." Jack winked at her. "Cheer up. Alejandro should be waiting for us."

– 20 –

Alejandro's Story, Part 1

"Gotta elevate my ankle." Jack's sore ankle throbbed from the combination of beach walking and climbing three flights of stairs to Jessica's condo.

Although the tension of their surprise encounter with Jessica's ex had subsided a bit, he made an effort to sweep away any lingering remnants of Ricky's dark cloud, focusing on the attractive distraction a couple steps above him as they climbed.

"Did you know the view from here is stunning?"

Jessica turned, peered down at Jack and wiggled her tush. "This the view you're talkin' about?"

"Me likey." He waggled his eyebrows.

"You're incorrigible."

Jessica unlocked the door and held it open for him. "Come on in, my poor, suffering, injured man."

The aroma of pipe smoke and the sound of hissing hit Jack the moment he crossed the threshold.

"Smells and sounds like we've got company."

Carrots, his back arched, was the source of the hiss, his usual sweet face stretched into an open-mouthed toothy sneer. He directed his ire at Alejandro's shimmering image, which hovered a couple inches above the kitchen floor. The pirate's dark eyes glimmered in the soft under-cabinet lighting. The cat spat and hissed his disapproval.

"Oh, my poor kitty. You haven't met Alejandro yet, have you?"

Carrots' aggressive stance abated at the sound of Jessica's voice, but his puffy tail still whipped back and forth.

A scowling Alejandro clamped down on his pipe stem with chipped and stained teeth. Wispy smoke drifted from the bowl to curl around his head.

He removed the pipe. "'Bout time ye showed up; yer cat scared th' bejesus outta me. Almost soiled meself."

Carrots stared at the ghost, as if issuing a final warning, then turned and ambled toward the bedroom, upright tail signaling victory.

Alejandro gazed at Jack as he tipped his head in Jessica's direction. "Got here early 'fore ye had a chance to drop yer anchor in 'er lagoon."

Jack rolled his eyes. "And a good evening to you too. What did I tell you about minding your language around the ladies?"

"No cursin' came outta me gob." The ghost's eyes widened, attempting to portray innocence.

"You're hopeless."

"You two are always at it," said Jessica. "Did you enjoy your tour of the cruise ship today, Alejandro?"

"Best time of me life... since bein' dead, 'at is. Found a lusty wench named Francine. Blew th' rust out of me pipes, she did."

Jessica laughed.

"Don't encourage him," Jack muttered. He turned toward the ghost. "You're unbelievable. I mean, how can you, um, even do it without a real..."

"Ye talkin' 'bout me hornpipe? Alejandro never disappoints th' wenches." He licked his pinky and smoothed an eyebrow. "Ye could take a few lessons from this old salt."

"I heard quite enough through the door of that stateroom. Don't need any lessons first-hand."

"Ya scurvy perv." The pirate scowled and leaned forward, hands on hips. "Listenin' outside th' door! Now, who's..."

"I think you owe me a story, Alejandro," said Jessica. "Remember, you promised to tell me all about my ancestors after your tour."

"Arrr. Rose Bodden. Th' most beautiful woman this Earth has ever seen, and th' love of me life." The ghost's eyes softened, taking on a dreamy quality. He pulled a gold pocket watch from his stained and tattered vest, squinting at the face. "Aye. Time's runnin' out. Gotta cross over soon."

"You can't leave until you tell your story." A little whine crept into Jessica's voice. "You promised."

"Got no control over th' time." The pirate glanced at the refrigerator. "How 'bout some grog to wet me whistle? Makes th' story-tellin' all th' better."

"A friendly warning," said Jack. "Beverages run right through him."

"What do you mean?" Jessica asked as she rummaged around inside the refrigerator for a beer.

"You'll see. Meanwhile, I'm going to have a seat at the table and prop up my injured foot."

"Ya stumble-bum." Alejandro snickered and drifted toward Jack. "One look at Rachel in th' pool and ye got tangled up in yer chair. No wonder th' wench left yer clumsy arse."

Jack elevated his foot on a vacant chair. "Ah, much better." He sighed, then turned to the insolent ghost. "Since you have *limited* time, why don't you cut the insults and tell your story?"

Jessica came to the table with three opened beers. "Might as well drink a beer with our friendly ghost."

The beer bottle levitated to Alejandro's mouth and then tipped, pouring the golden liquid down his gullet. The beer passed through his ghostly body, splattering on chair and floor.

"Ain't grog, ain't rum, but it ain't bad." He thumped his chest with his fist and emitted a loud belch.

"You're making a mess!" Jessica's eyes widened.

"I warned you." Jack sighed again, shaking his head.

"Ah, got me a glow goin'. 'Tis story time."

"Tell me about Rose Bodden, the love of your life." Jessica perched on the edge of her chair, ignoring the beer slick on the floor.

"I told ye when me first met Rose Bodden, I was face down in th' sand, bleedin' and gaspin' fer me breath. Blackbeard 'ad just sunk me ship and told me t' swim t' shore like th' filthy bilge rat I was."

"Yes, I remember. That's where the story stopped."

"Ah, me Rose. Always helpin' somebody—even this filthy ol' pirate. Seein' me half dead, she pulled out 'er 'andkerchief—smelled like roses—mopped me face, dabbed at me bloody wounds, and 'elped me stand."

"Was she a fine lady—you know, like an aristocrat?"

"Aye. She was high born. Rose was shipped 'ere to live wit' 'er uncle, Mr. Bodden. Ya see, she wasn't married but had a baby—scandalous, back then. 'Er parents thought she'd stay outta trouble on this God-forsaken island. Back in 1715, this ol' limestone rock was no vacation spot. It offered nothin' but rough livin'. Mosquitoes th' size of bats. Heat so wretched in th' summer, likely curdle yer guts. Few souls lived 'ere back then."

"After she helped you, did she take you home with her?" Jessica leaned forward, hanging on the ghost's every word.

"Aye. I could barely walk, mind ya. She took me to 'er home, proppin' me up all the way. When 'er uncle saw me, he 'bout blew a nut. Ragin' on 'bout bringin' a lawless piece o' dung into 'is home. Well, Rose would 'ave none of 'at talk. She told 'im he was a sorry excuse fer th' righteous upstandin' Christian man he claimed to be."

"Good for her. I admire a girl with some sass."

"She 'ad plenty o' that. Th' next thing me remembers is wakin' up a day later in a bed wit' fine linens, bandages on me wounds, an' bollock naked under th' covers. And peekin' at me from th' doorway was a wee girl. This buccaneer didn't wanna cause no further trouble, so me smiled at th' little lass. Seemed to be all th' encouragement she needed. Skipped over to me bed and stared at me wit' eyes round as doubloons, then whispered, 'Are you th' thieving scoundrel that washed ashore?'"

The ghost pointed his pipe at Jessica. "Mind ya, now, me always had a soft spot for th' young scalawags, so me winked and nodded. She edged a bit closer and asked, 'What did you steal?'"

"Told 'er me stole th' hearts of pretty young women. She laughed and called me a silly flibbertigibbet. 'Bout this time, Rose charged into th' room. Ya see, th' lass was Rose's daughter. Violet was her name. Pretty as a picture, bold as brass.

"Rose scolded Violet for botherin' me, but 'twas likely she was a bit suspicious of me mangy arse, what wit' her snivelin' uncle fillin' 'er head wit' fearful tales."

"Well, pirates are dangerous." Jessica raised an eyebrow.

"Aye. But a little girl 'as nothin' to fear from me. Whaddaya take me for?"

"No insult intended. When did Rose fall in love with you? What happened to little Violet? Did you have any children with Rose?"

"Just gettin' to that, missy. Yer rushin' th' story."

"Sorry. I'll shut up so you can talk."

"See 'at ya do. Time's runnin' shooorrrttt…" Alejandro's voice trailed off into silence. His image flickered like an old-fashioned black-and-white TV, and he vanished.

"Oh no! This can't be." Jessica grabbed at the air as if to retrieve the ghost. She tugged on Jack's arm. "Do something! Make him come back."

– 21 –

Alejandro Delivers a Message

Ricky polished the lenses of his binoculars with the hem of his tee shirt while pacing the dark beach, contemplating his next move. He reminded himself that knowledge was power. Meeting Jack stoked his rage, but now he knew what he was up against: just another American on vacation hooking up with a local. *A temporary problem.*

Since their divorce, Ricky had felt confident Jessica would come to her senses, eventually, and want him back in his rightful place as her husband. He grimaced. Now, that once-rock-solid assumption was starting to wobble like a tower of Jell-o. He'd monitored Jack and Jessica's journey to the Calypso Grill via the GPS tracker app on his phone. They'd spent two hours there, and he wound himself up taut as a tightrope, imagining them simpering at each other over a long, drawn-out romantic dinner.

When the two returned to the condo complex, he followed them to the beach and stalked them from a distance, until finally choosing the perfect moment to reveal himself. He chuckled, reliving the scene. *Not always in charge are ya, Jessica?*

The thought occurred to him that Jessica might be going off the rails. Taking up with some wonky dude who mentioned a meeting with a ghost.... Nonsense talk, the kind of talk he'd heard all his life from older native islanders. Beliefs in duppies and spirits were steeped in their African and Jamaican roots.

It was past time for the oldsters to drop their superstitions. There was still a sign on the north end of the island marking a bend in the road as "Duppy Turn," since many locals claimed they saw ghosts or duppies in the area. Legend had it pirates buried their treasures there, then killed and buried local Caymanian slaves to "guard" their wealth.

Normally, he made fun of the ridiculous stories. However, recent events gave him pause. He hadn't been able to explain what really happened a couple nights ago, when his binoculars somehow lifted from around his neck and smashed themselves against the stucco building. Top that off with a rough voice whispering a warning in his ear: he'd freaked out, stumbling backwards into the prickly bougainvillea bush. There was still a thorn embedded deep in his palm, painful and festering. Another thorn had been forking out three hundred dollars for new binoculars.

Ricky plodded through the sand, eager to continue his surveillance. Just imagining what Jack was doing in Jessica's condo torqued him. *That prick's probably fucking my wife.* He made a guttural sound, followed by the whispered proclamation, "I oughta kill 'em both."

The aroma of pipe smoke wafted under his nose. Then, suddenly, he was attacked from behind, his hot rage turning to icy fear in an instant. The binoculars flipped over; the straps twisted and tightened around his neck, making an effective garrote. He panicked and wildly kicked out, connecting only with the night's balmy air. The pressure increased. He pawed at the straps digging into his flesh and prayed for a breath of precious air. Flickering lights obscured his vision. His bladder let loose, soaking his pants. He slumped onto the sand. Blackness covered him like a sodden wool blanket.

A sharp kick to his kidneys brought him around. His eyelids fluttered as his brain scrambled to catch up.

"Am I dead?" He could barely croak out the question.

"Me wishes ya was dead, ya steamin' heap o' dog shit. Shoulda hung ya by yer nutmegs."

Ricky clutched his neck, instinctively assessing the damage. Satisfied his head was still attached to his body, he swallowed. Pain seared his throat, and he coughed, ushering in a round of amped-up agony. Fear and anger coursed through him. Attempting an assertive voice, he only managed a raspy whimper. "Who are you?"

Another blast of pipe smoke hit him in the face. He coughed again and rolled over in the sand, sprawled out like a rag doll. Sinister laughter from the disembodied voice washed over his prone body.

"This ol' buccaneer's a friend. But not *yer* friend. Listen up, ya thick-headed lard-brain. Leave Jack and Jessica alone. Take yer scabby arse and leave th' island."

Ricky nodded.

"Not sure ya understand."

A heavy weight landed on his torso, squeezing the air from his lungs. It felt like a car was parked on his chest. He tried to push away the weight, but his hands just passed through thin air.

"*Adios. Hasta nunca,* Ricky."

Alejandro's spirit hovered over Ricky, who lay unconscious and curled up on the sand in a fetal position. *Ya maggot-infested carp, wastin' me time wit' yer interferin' sneaky ways.* The ghost's energy was flagging; his image had disappeared. Inflicting harm on the living came at a high price.

He'd been enjoying his evening, feeding on Jessica's enthusiasm, when the overwhelming sensation of Ricky's negative energy interrupted his storytelling and pulled him away. Alejandro had no choice but to crack down on Ricky for wreaking havoc and disrupting his plan. He was so close to accomplishing his two remaining tasks—one task really, as the fates had woven them together over time.

The ghost's challenge was to balance his remaining energy with the time he had left. Once his tasks were completed, he could cross over. His soul longed to be reunited with Rose. Bound to the oath he'd made to her three hundred years ago, he would die a thousand times over to keep his promise. And Ricky had cost him plenty tonight.

His right hand itched for his cutlass so he could separate Ricky's head from his body. A permanent solution, but the energy expended for an act of murder would bankrupt him. He'd dealt Ricky a sound thrashing, and hoped it was enough to keep him away from Jessica and Jack.

The greatest pirate to ever sail the Caribbean needed to rest and restore as best he could. Alejandro caught a whiff of roses as he drifted off.

– 22 –

Revelations

"I wish I could summon Alejandro for you, but I can't control him. Maybe he'll show up tomorrow night." Jack reached for Jessica's hand across the table and gave it a squeeze. As much as he liked playing the role of Super Boyfriend, he couldn't pull this trick out of his hat.

"He was in the middle of his story—he can't leave me hanging."

"Call out his name, maybe he'll come back. He likes the ladies, especially the pretty ones. Well, you're prettier when you're smiling."

Jessica dropped her pouty frown and produced a little smile. "Perhaps, but Alejandro favors you because you remind him of his own brother. What was his name ... Javier?"

"So he said." Jack shrugged.

"He appeared the very first night you were here, and has been hanging around ever since. I think you're his project."

"What about the story of your ancestors?" asked Jack. "That's all for you."

"That part is. But Alejandro keeps spicing up your life. Ya gotta admit it's been a crazy, action-packed five days." Her eyes narrowed. "An idea just hit me. Do you suppose you *are* Javier, Alejandro's reincarnated brother?"

"What? That's crazy."

"Maybe not. That would explain his behavior—his focus on you."

"I don't know, Jessica. Sounds far-fetched. However, I think he's playing matchmaker."

Jessica nodded. "Alejandro definitely played a role in throwing us together."

"He encouraged me to talk to you at Pirate Night at the bar next door." Jack paused. "I'll show you."

Jack stood and pantomimed smoking a pipe, mimicking the pirate's stance. "'Git over there and impress 'er with yer razor-sharp wit. If that don't work, buy 'er that fancy rum drink.'"

Jessica laughed. "You sound exactly like him!"

"That's because I've been spending way too much time with him." Jack stretched and flexed his ankle. "Let's move to the sofa. I need a cushier seat."

They sunk into the overstuffed couch with Jack's foot propped on the coffee table. "Much better. Plus, I get to have my arm around you."

"Our friendly ghost acts like a man on a mission. He appears regularly, and is always roping you, or us, into doing something for him." Jessica snuggled into Jack, leaning her head on his shoulder. "Speaking of Pirate Night, he seemed to know we were in danger when he came to our aid on the beach."

"If he knew that, I wonder if Alejandro knows Ricky's stalking us?"

"Good point. If we ever see him again, we'll ask. Wouldn't that be wild if he"—she used finger quotes—"'took care of Ricky' for me?"

"Be careful what you wish for. We don't want Ricky to be murdered by a ghost, do we?" No response, so Jack nudged Jessica for an answer.

"Okay. Not murdered, but removed from the island. I'd be happy with that."

"Oh my God. I just figured it out." Jack stiffened. He felt the mental puzzle pieces interlocking.

"Figured what out?"

"Your ring. Ricky stole your opal ring."

"What in God's name are you talking about? I'm wearing my ring." She wiggled her fingers in Jack's line of vision.

"Your ring was missing for a while, but you didn't know it."

"And how would *you* know about that?" Jessica frowned and pulled away from Jack.

Jack fixed his stare across the room on a framed print of ragged cliffs jutting upwards at a 90-degree angle from roiling seas. He felt the tingling sensation of standing on a wobbly rock at the cliff's edge.

The week's bizarre events had piled up, and now were converging. *A pirate ghost has been meddling in my life. Jessica is coincidentally linked to that ghost by her ancestral past. And now Ricky; jealous, maybe a dangerous stalker. And what about crossing paths with Rachel on the cruise ship?* Jack closed his eyes and wondered how an even-keeled, steady-Eddy like himself ever got caught up in such mystery, danger, and romance.

He'd fallen in love with a woman in five days. *What do I really know about her? How could she have hooked up with a train wreck like Ricky? Yes, he changed after they were married, but still ... and, since his home's Grand Cayman, will we ever be rid of him?*

The irony wasn't lost on Jack. How could he judge anybody's relationship mistakes after he'd been ditched on his wedding day? But the red devil on his shoulder whispered, *At least Rachel's not a dangerous stalker.* He muted the negative voice. Jessica wasn't responsible for Ricky's behavior, plain and simple.

He met Jessica's gaze. The perplexed look on her face squeezed his heart. He loved her, and resented any interference from a tool like Ricky.

"I've got one helluva story for you, if you want to hear it."

He stroked the back of her hand with his thumb. "Interested? Or do you want to throw me out?"

"I'll admit I'm confused—feel like I'm totally in the dark. But my supposedly missing ring is on my finger, and my instincts tell me you're not a bad guy or a thief. So, let's hear it."

Jack launched into his story, starting with waking up the previous morning to the opal ring on his bedside stand. Jessica remained silent as the tale unfolded, ending with Jack seeing the ring on her finger when she came over for dinner.

"Aha! So that's why your clothes were strewn all over the bedroom floor. You were digging for the ring."

"That's your first comment? Not, 'Who the hell stole my ring?'"

"Still trying to process that." She furrowed her brow. "It's very disturbing."

"Naturally—or rather supernaturally—I figured Alejandro was to blame. He popped in while I put the finishing touches on dinner that night, when you were out on the screened-in porch. He acted all pissed off when I blamed him for stealing your ring, saying he didn't appreciate me 'accusin' him of high crimes.' In fact, he told me he was responsible for returning the ring to you."

"This story gets crazier by the moment," said Jessica. "Alejandro didn't explain?"

"No. I asked him who stole the ring, but he didn't answer. He just commented that I had bigger problems, and to keep 'a sharp eye out.' Then he disappeared."

"Ricky's got to be the culprit behind the ring." Jessica wrapped her arms around herself and scowled.

"How could he possibly pull that off? He would've had to get into your condo, remove the ring, and then sneak into my condo to put it on my bedside stand. That's a lot of risky prowling around."

"Shortly after we split, Ricky lost his job. Trying to be helpful,

I hired him as the night shift security guard for this condo complex. That meant he had a master key—part of the job."

"You gave Ricky a job?" Jack rolled his eyes. "That's going above and beyond. What were you thinking?"

"You don't get to be critical, Jack, just listen. At the time, I felt obligated to help him because I thought the stress of our divorce was contributing to his downward spiral."

"Let me guess," said Jack, "you eventually had to fire him."

"I did. People complained he was over-zealous in his job, stopping residents for just walking around the property at night. Also, one of our elderly residents claimed money had been stolen from her condo. I had no proof he was the thief, but it was time for him to go regardless. He turned in the master key, but he could've had a key made for himself."

"He must be quite a cat burglar, breaking in like that without waking you or me."

"I often leave my ring on the kitchen counter; a bad habit. He wouldn't make much noise just opening the door, stepping in and grabbing the ring. As for you, you must be a sound sleeper."

"The more we talk over the strange events of the last few days, the more I believe Ricky's a serious problem. Alejandro could probably fill in the blanks if he'd only show up again."

"It's late, and I'm exhausted." Jessica rubbed her eyes and yawned. "Not to mention a little bit scared and a lot angry. I want Ricky out of my life."

"Let's call it a night." Jack pulled Jessica close to him and kissed her. "Tomorrow morning, we'll check to see if there's a tracking device on your car. In the meantime, remember, you're safe with me."

"Only two nights left. No time to waste."

"I thought you were exhausted?"

"Yes, but not comatose. Take me to bed."

– 23 –

Discovery

"Hey, pal. You okay?"

An intense light penetrated Ricky's eyelids, rousting him from his hypnogogic state. He raised his arm to obstruct the visual assault, triggering a wave of pain that kept him pinned to the sand.

"Well, you're alive anyway," said the man. "Nearly stumbled over you."

The light shifted away from Ricky's eyes. He squinted, a geezer wearing a headlamp and carrying a metal detector resolving into view.

"Need help?" The man extended his hand.

Ricky grabbed it and tried to stand, but lost his balance and slumped back to the sand. His body felt like it'd been through a meat grinder.

"From what I can see, you don't look so good. Want me to call an ambulance?"

"No. No ambulance," Ricky muttered, hoarsely. "Just go away."

The man crouched. "I can't leave you here. You need medical attention."

The stranger's concern made Ricky's skin prickle with annoyance. "Yeah, and what are you? A goddamned doctor?" He winced from the effort of speaking. Every word felt like a stab in his throat.

"Retired pediatrician, actually. What happened to you?"

"Too much to drink," lied Ricky.

Of course, Ricky recalled the attack, which he finally had to admit was administered by a ghost. *Must be some kind of powerful evil spirit.* He felt at his throat, wondering if there'd be permanent damage to his vocal cords. He didn't relish the idea of croaking out his words, frog-like, for the rest of his life.

"It's six o'clock in the morning—you been laying here all night?"

"Now you're a detective?" Ricky wondered what it would take to get the Good Samaritan asshole to move along. "Why can't you old people mind your own fucking business?"

"At least let me help you stand." The good doctor grabbed Ricky under the arms and helped pull him up. Ricky fought off a rush of nausea as he struggled to remain on his feet. He spotted his binoculars partially buried in the sand.

He pointed and said, "Gimme those." The man obliged. Ricky turned and started a slow slog down the dark beach, binoculars in hand. No way was that strap going around his neck anytime soon.

The stranger adjusted his headlamp and called out, "I'll keep an eye on you to make sure you're okay. I'm just sweeping the beach looking for lost treasures. Nothing that can't be interrupted. Go see a doctor… soon."

Ricky gave the guy the finger. What he needed was an exorcist, not a fucking doctor. He'd be damned if he'd let some ghost push him around, warning him to leave the island. *I'll send you straight back to the hell you came from.*

His false bravado was a veil masking his fear—still there, but fuzzy around the edges. He had no idea how to combat a ghost. Hard to fight something you can't see. Stranger still, the ghost demanded that he leave Jessica alone. This, shortly after Jack commented he and Jessica had a meeting with a ghost. Something was afoot, and Ricky was drawn to it like a toddler to a choking hazard.

"Found it!" Jack crawled out from underneath Jessica's Prius clutching a magnetic GPS tracker smaller than a deck of cards. With the aid of a powerful penlight, he'd discovered it stuck to the inside of the wheel well.

"What a dickhead," said Jessica. "I'd really hoped you wouldn't find anything."

"You calling me a dickhead?" Jack asked as he brushed parking lot dirt from his shirt.

"No. Ricky. Who else? Now, what'll I do?"

"If you want to mess with him, we can attach the tracker to a garbage truck. He'll have fun chasing it around the island looking for your car."

"Tempting," said Jessica, "and a little bit funny, but I'm really concerned about this whole thing."

"Come on. Let's put this device in your condo for safe keeping." Jack took Jessica's hand, and they headed toward the stairs. "Ricky's a stalker, pure and simple, and he has to be stopped. Go to the police, and show them that tracker. They'll know what to do. In fact, I'll go with you."

"It's your last day here, and I don't want to spend it dealing with all this Ricky crap." Jessica unlocked and opened the door to her condo. They stepped inside. "It's like he wins if he disrupts our time together."

"I understand," said Jack, "but I want to make sure you're safe before I leave. And getting the police involved is a step in the right direction."
"I promise I'll go directly to the police station tomorrow morning after I drop you off at the airport." Jessica pressed Jack against the wall. "There are far better ways to spend the day."

She snuck her hand between them, exploring below his waist with a teasing, feathery touch. Jack's body reacted, his mind filling with ways to please her. A long-distance relationship demanded every second together be treasured, and the clock was ticking away like Big Ben, large and loud.

"You're right," said Jack. "Only one thing comes to my mind."

He gathered her close and breathed in the clean scent of her skin and hair, storing the sensations in his brain so they could be enjoyed later, when he was on that big silver bird jetting back to reality.

The thought of being apart from her caused a hitch in his heart, firing his passion. His gaze shifted from her dark brown eyes to her mouth. She tilted her head back and parted her lips. Jack accepted the unspoken invitation, covering her mouth with his in a sweet, lingering kiss. His hands slipped down to her waist, and still lower, until he was caressing her rounded bottom. Jessica slowly rotated her hips, pushing into his erection. Her kisses became greedy, as if he was her lifeline.

Overcome with desire, Jack broke away from her kiss. He unbuttoned her white, sleeveless blouse, exposing a lacy pink bra beneath. The crushing urge to rush to the orgasmic prize at the end almost overwhelmed him. Seizing the few threads of restraint he had left, he paced himself and gently traced the outline of her bra with his finger, captivated by her smooth skin in contrast with the raised texture of the lace. Finally, he allowed his thumb to slip inside and brush against her nipple.

With a sharp intake of breath, Jessica closed her eyes at Jack's touch. She tugged on the tie of his board shorts, loosening them to run her hands along his narrow, bare hips, working her way to the front. When she gripped the center of his universe, he kicked all restraint to the curb.

A trail of clothes littered the floor from the front door to the bedroom; last to go was the pink lacy bra.

– 24 –

The Pool Guy

Ricky awoke on the narrow couch in Leon Scott's apartment late in the morning, hot and miserable. *No air conditioning in this shitty place.* His sweat contributed to the funky odor of the sofa's upholstery. Nightmares of ghosts chasing him on a dark beach had plagued his short, sketchy sleep. The apparitions resembled vaporous blobs, with vague, wispy appendages and a black hole where their mouths might've been. He'd tried to run, but the soft sand bogged him down until he dropped from exhaustion. The clammy touch of the ghosts' hands around his neck had jarred him awake.

"Hey man, you up? We gotta be to work in an hour." Ricky opened one eye, nostrils flaring at the sweet, cloying aroma of pot smoke. Leon's face came into view, a lit fat-boy dangling from his lips.

"Where the fuck were you last night?" asked Leon. He took a deep drag on the joint, exhaled a pungent, blue-tinged cloud of smoke, and held out a mug. "Here. Fresh coffee."

Ricky gingerly sat up. The movement produced a chain of aches and pains. He suppressed a groan and grasped the mug.

"Thanks, man." Those two words confirmed his worse suspicions. The frog-like voice was the new norm for a while, if not forever.

"Dude, you sound like shit. What happened to your voice?" Leon frowned and held out the joint. "Wanna hit?"

"No. Might be a virus, laryngitis, or some such bullshit."

"So, where were you last night? Must've been some rough pussy the way you look … and smell."

"Nowhere special."

"Okay. 'Nuff said. A dude's gotta have his privacy."

Leon pasted a cheery smile on his face and pulled his dreadlocks into a ponytail, securing them with a rubber band. "So, how much longer do you think you'll need to stay here, anyways?"

Ricky knew where this was going. They both worked at Mister Splash Pool Service, and Leon had reluctantly agreed to let him stay at his cramped apartment. Ricky suspected the company owner, desperate for employees, had monetarily incented Leon to accommodate him. But, apparently not enough to buy even a half-assed window air conditioner. He mopped the sweat from his face with his tee shirt.

"Don't know." Ricky frowned. "Gotta save up so I can afford my own place. Takes time."

"You lived with your mom before, right?"

"Yeah. Can't go back there, though. She's like living with an exposed nerve. Always ridin' my ass."

After Jessica pulled the plug on his pool business and kicked him out, his piss-poor financial situation forced him to move in with his mother. She blamed him for his failed marriage, suggested he get his shit together, and specified that furthering his education would be a good start. Pamphlets for a trade school in Florida showed up on the kitchen table and on his bedroom dresser. Just because he'd installed a new light fixture for her, she'd concluded he had a natural aptitude for electricity.

"Do you have any other family?" asked Leon. "I mean, you grew up on this island, right?"

"I did. Look, Leon, I know you're trying to get rid of me, but I got nowhere to go right now. My divorce left me dead-ass broke."

"Dude. Sorry. Didn't know about any divorce."

Ricky sensed an opportune time to play the victim card. "I went to a trade school in Florida to become an electrician, but found out I had to work as an apprentice for four years before I could become licensed. Four years of being someone's go-fer. Fuck that shit, you know?"

Leon nodded in understanding. "I hear ya. That would suck."

"Exactly. So, I came back here to get my ex back."

"She interested?" Leon re-lit his joint and took another hit.

"Maybe. She tried to help me out after we split. Hired me as a security guard at the condos she manages. Then, some old hag accused me of stealing her money, a whopping fifty dollars—like that's such a big-ass deal. So, my ex believed her and kicked me to the curb… again."

"Doesn't sound good. You sure you want 'er back?"

"If you saw her, you'd get it. Today we're cleaning the pools where she works. Anyway, if I could just hang out here for a couple more weeks…"

Ricky stood and stretched his achy muscles. Nausea churned his guts. "Gotta shower now. We good here?"

"Sure. A couple more weeks; no problem."

Control was slipping from Ricky's grasp. He'd hit a new low sucking up to a loser like Leon. He trudged into the bathroom, dreading his reflection in the mirror. To his relief, there was no visible bruising around his neck. *That fucking ghost—didn't even leave a mark.* Fear and anger ran a tight race through his veins. Anger crossed the finish line first, sparking a revelation so obvious it made Ricky laugh. The root of all his problems? Jessica. She controlled this pet ghost of hers like a vindictive puppet master, dancing him around on her personal stage, carrying out her evil deeds. He rubbed his throat. *Paybacks are a bitch, bitch.*

Ricky opened the linen closet. He pawed through the jumble of hand towels and washcloths, searching for a clean bath towel. The only one left was in the very back of the cabinet. He grabbed it and paused, feeling something hard and weighty. He laid the towel on the counter and unfolded it, revealing a handgun.

Like his first day on the island, Jack settled into the same chair on the same patch of sand. He tilted the beach umbrella to provide maximum shade. The cooler, filled with Caybrew, sat within easy reach. He'd just delivered the good news about Caribbean Marine to his boss. The boat dealer called Jack an hour ago and gave him a purchase order number for two boats, one for their showroom and one for stock. Noble Yachts could quickly fill the gap in Caribbean Marine's product offerings. The opportunity for more business was ripe.

Jack dreaded tomorrow morning, when a flight would take him away from Jessica and the sunny island for his job and snowy Michigan. His cock stiffened at the thought of her. Their intense lovemaking this morning left him sated, but the overwhelming need would return. With Jessica, he felt complete, like he was home. He'd loathed the thought of the long wait until he could see her again in April. *Does absence make the heart fonder, or wander?* But the new business opportunity demanded he return sooner. Jack smiled. *A win-win.* He wasn't about to lose Jessica due to distance or time.

Jack's thoughts turned to the Ricky issue. He pondered how dangerous Jessica's ex could be. *Is he just a creepy stalker, or will he try to physically harm Jessica? She promised to go to the police with the GPS tracker, but can they really protect her?* He suspected Alejandro knew far more about Ricky then he'd let on. *But is the ghost willing or able to protect her?* Moot questions if the pirate had already crossed over, leaving Jessica on her own to combat the Ricky menace. Jack didn't care much for that scenario. He found himself hoping the ghost would return.

Jack checked the time. Jessica had promised to meet him on the beach around three o'clock when she finished working. He turned and looked toward her condo, noticing a couple of men dressed in white clothing cleaning the pool. Hats with attached fabric sun shields covered the backs of their necks, as well as their faces from the nose down. Wrap-around sunglasses nearly covered the rest of their faces. A toolkit labeled Mister Splash Pool Service sat between them.

It was nearly three o'clock, so Jack headed toward Jessica's condo, hoping to meet her coming his way. When he passed the workmen, one of them dropped the skimmer he was using, turned toward Jack, and muttered something.

"Excuse me?" Jack paused.

"Good afternoon." The man's voice was raspy. He reached for his skimming net and resumed working.

"Oh, same to you." Jack continued walking and felt water sprinkle his back. He spun around in time to see the man put the skimmer back into the water.

Did he intentionally splash me? Jack shook his head. He immediately forgot the incident when he spotted Jessica coming down the stairs from her condo. He hurried to greet her, hoping the white, turquoise-beaded bikini lurked underneath her beach cover-up.

"Hey, how was work?" He took her beach bag and draped his arm around her shoulders. They strolled side-by-side on the walkway leading to the ocean.

"The best part about work was knowing I'd get to see you

at the end of my day." Jessica leaned in and kissed Jack on the cheek. "I could get used to this."

"Used to what?"

"Having you around, you knucklehead."

"That must mean you're falling for me."

"A strong possibility."

"You'll be super impressed when you see the sweet spot I staked out on the beach. An umbrella *and* a cooler of cold Caybrews."

"Such service. Are you like this all the time? Sweet, thoughtful, and, I have to throw this in, an amazing lover. Or is this Vacation Jack?" Jessica reached behind and squeezed his butt.

"I'm like this all the time. The only vacation part of me is the SPF 50 sunscreen."

"You are kind of white." Jessica chuckled. "A few more days in the sun, and you'll look more like me. What do ya say?" She held her arm next to his, comparing their skin colors.

"I'd love to stay a few more days. But I've got this pesky thing called a job that needs my attention."

Jessica stopped just short of the pool. She stood on her tiptoes, kissed Jack, and whispered, "I don't want you to leave."

"You said that yesterday."

"I know. It's even truer now. Especially since this morning."

"Well, then, I have some good news for you. I'll be returning before April. Caribbean Marine ordered two boats today."

"Oh, Jack. Congratulations! How exciting is that?" She wrapped her arms around him and gave him a big squeeze, then looked up at him with a sideways glance. "You always this successful?"

"Of course. One call is all it takes."

"Are you bragging?"

"Ain't braggin' if it's true." Jack grinned.

Jessica waggled her eyebrows. "We should celebrate."

"Keep talking like that, and we'll never get to the beach."

Before Jessica could respond, one of the pool workers approached them. Jack nudged her. "I think this guy has a question."

She turned and asked, "Hi. Can I help you with something?"

The man pulled off his hat and sun shield to reveal Ricky's face, pinched and angry-looking. "Well, hello, Jessica." He coughed like he was trying to clear the croak in his voice.

"You again?" Jessica scowled. "What are you doing here?"

"Should be obvious, my darling wife. Cleaning the pool. Trying to keep everything nice and pretty for all the *vacationers.* Like Jack here. Isn't it about time your holiday ended, pal? Time to go back to wherever the fuck you came from?"

"Ricky, shut up," said Jessica. "So you work for Mister Splash now? Do your job and leave. I have nothing to say to you. Come on, Jack, let's go."

Jack flexed his still-sore right hand. *Is it worth popping this fucker?* He relished the idea of Ricky's nose bleeding all over his white uniform, and took a deep breath. "Thought we covered this last night," said Jack in a low tone, "but maybe it didn't sink in. Leave. Jessica. Alone." He poked Ricky in the chest. "She doesn't want your sorry ass in her life. Got it?"

Ricky belted out a raspy laugh. "Right-o, Jack. Not the first time I've heard that message. Have a marvelous fucking day."

He turned and sauntered back to the pool.

"I'm so tired of running into this fool," said Jack.

"Same here," said Jessica. "I know you set up a great spot on the beach, but I don't wanna hang out there knowing Ricky can watch us."

"I hear ya. I'll pack up the beach stuff, and we'll do something else."

"Actually, there's a special place I'd love to show you—the Cayman Crystal Caves. I had put it on the back burner for your return trip, but if we hurry we can catch the last tour of the day."

"Caves?" asked Jack. "As in, stalagmites and stalactites?"

Jessica nodded. "The caves have an eerie and mysterious vibe, but they also possess a pristine natural beauty you won't find anywhere else."

"Sounds like Alejandro's kind of place."

"Maybe back in the day. Legend says pirates used to hide their treasure in the caves."

"Has any treasure ever been found?" asked Jack.

"I don't know." Jessica shrugged. "The locals have known about these caves forever, so maybe people have found things."

"Let's go." Jack chuckled. "Ricky will be so disappointed when he can't track us."

– 25 –

The Caves

Jessica rolled to a stop in the deserted parking lot, tires making crunching sounds in the loose gravel. The ticket window's shade was drawn down; a sign reading Closed dangled by a string, swaying listless in the balmy breeze.

"Nobody's here?" asked Jack.

"The last tour's at 4:00, and it's only 3:45."

"Maybe they didn't have any customers, so just knocked off for the day?"

"I should've called ahead, but ... we were in a hurry."

"They would've given the tour to only two people?"

"Sure. It's a laid-back place. Not like touring Mammoth Cave in the States."

"Can we explore on our own?"

"We're not supposed to." Jessica glanced around. "But ... I don't see any security guards anywhere."

"Wanna give it a try?"

"Why not? The gate's closed, but we could walk around it."

"I'm up for another adventure," said Jack. "If we get caught, I'll tell the authorities you lured me here with promises of pirate treasure."

"That's it. Throw me under the bus."

Jack got out of the car. A raucous squawking sounded from above, making him jump. "Hey, what's that sound?"

"Parrots. Look up in that almond tree." Jessica shut her car door. "They blend in with the leaves."

Jack watched the bustling parrots, guessing there to be at least a hundred of them, mostly green with some red feathers fringing their faces and necks. "The only time I've ever seen a parrot is in a cage."

"They're endangered and, thankfully, protected."

Jack took Jessica's hand. "Lead the way, Madame Tour Director."

They skirted the gate and picked up the path leading toward the caves. "Normally a van drives visitors to the first cave, but ah, we're breaking in, so it's about a mile walk. Your ankle okay with that?"

"Sure. Remember, I'm a tough guy." As if his ankle had ears, it sent a warning shot up to Jack's brain in the form of jabbing pains. He turned his head to hide his wince from Jessica. "Tell me about the caves."

"A real tour guide could tell you more, but you're stuck with me. In total, there are a little over a hundred caves. Three of them have been carefully excavated, and were opened to the public about four years ago. The best one is the Lake Cave. We'll go there first, before we run out of daylight."

They continued down the rustic path, lined with jumbo-sized plants and wild fig trees, all competing for space and sunlight. The parrots were engaged in a full-out fracas, flitting from tree to tree, shaking branches and rustling leaves.

Jack put his arm around Jessica's waist and pulled her close. "A spooky place. Dirt trail, dense tropical forest... maybe some ghosts."

"Ha. Like we need another ghost."

Jack spotted a mammoth plant and paused, feigning interest to give his smarting ankle a break. "Look, Jessica. This aloe is as tall as me."

"That's actually an agave plant." Jessica grinned. "Where tequila comes from."

"What I wouldn't do for a margarita right now... and a chair," muttered Jack.

Jessica pointed. "Just ahead. See the sign?"

"Reminds me of the sign in The Haunted Forest," said Jack, walking up to a piece of hand-lettered driftwood. "'Welcome to Lake Cave.' Maybe it should say, 'I'd Turn Back If I Were You!'"

"Funny guy. Are you a *Wizard of Oz* fan?" asked Jessica.

"My mom took me to see the movie when I was a little kid. Scared the crap out of me."

"No need to be scared now." Jessica winked. "You're safe with me."

"I doubt that." He gestured toward the cave's entrance. "After you."

"Don't touch anything," said Jessica as she entered the cave.

"Not even you?"

Jessica looked over her shoulder and rolled her eyes. Jack followed her in. "Whoa. This place looks like another planet—it's surreal. These formations are amazing." He removed his sunglasses so he could see in the dim interior. "They light these caves?"

"Yes. The lights are strategically placed so you can see the different cave-scapes. Look at this one." Jessica pointed to a stalactite, about fifteen feet long, protruding from the ceiling. "Notice the little stalactite that formed within this stalactite. Very rare."

"It's even more humid in here than outside." The cave glistened with moisture that clung to every surface. Jack's skin and cotton clothing absorbed the damp. He took a deep breath, surprised that the air smelled fresh and clean. *Thought it'd stink like my grandma's moldy attic.* He glanced up and studied the ceiling, crowded with stalactites of various lengths and girths.

"What a bizarre place. It's weirdly quiet, like a sound-proofed room."

"My cousins played in these caves when they were kids, long before any excavation took place," said Jessica. "They crawled in from access holes in the ground."

"Paradise for a kid," said Jack. "I'll bet their imaginations ran wild in this eerie place. Did you ever go with them?"

"Nah. I was too young…and scared. Being boys, they teased me by telling me the caves were full of ghosts." Jessica laughed. "They were probably right about that. Ready to see the lake? It's an impressive sight."

"Sure."

They continued on the winding path, pebble-strewn and surrounded by odd formations. Some stalagmites, growths rising from the cave's floor, looked like stacks of donuts coated in powdered diamond instead of sugar, while others resembled pointy witch's fingers.

Jack ducked, wincing as a drip of water hit his head and trickled down the back of his shirt. "Can it rain inside a cave?"

"You caught a drop? That means you'll have seven years of good luck."

"You could be a tour guide here," said Jack.

"It's customary to tip the tour guide."

"Oh, I've gotta tip for you."

"Watch yourself. You could get kicked off of the tour, and then where would you be?"

"Lost?"

"That's right. Look ahead," said Jessica.

"An underground lake," Jack murmured. "Incredible."

They approached the aquamarine-colored body of water, still and clear as gin, and sat on a flat rock at the pool's edge. Poking down from the cave's ceiling hung dozens of cream-colored stalactites, some so long they penetrated the lake's utterly still surface.

"A person couldn't stand up in this lake; they'd be skewered," remarked Jack.

"I know. Some of these formations look like swords," said Jessica.

Shadows made the cave-scapes surrounding the lake look sinister, as if the formations could spring to life at any moment. Jack tried to imagine life in the 1700s. What kind of nefarious activities had happened in this cave? Buried treasure? Buried bodies? Romantic—and not so romantic—hook-ups? He shook off his day-dreaming and asked Jessica, "How big is this lake?"

"About six hundred feet long. And it's fresh water."

"Unbelievable. Does anyone ever swim in it?" He pictured the two of them, all alone in this strange setting, skinny-dipping in the subterranean lake.

"Not allowed," said Jessica. "Why? You tempted to wade in?"

"No way. Might be quicksand in there."

"You have an active imagination." Jessica grinned and took Jack's hand.

"You ever been kissed in this cave?" He smiled back at her, loving how the soft hair framing her face curled in the humid air.

"No. I haven't."

"We'll have to fix that." He gathered her close and barely brushed her lips with his, then pulled back. She lightly traced his mouth with her finger.

"Kiss me, Jack."

His teeth grazed her lower lip, and her soft mouth parted to accept his kiss. He felt her tongue scarcely touch his. Jack's hand slipped down to her breast. He caressed her through the gauzy fabric of her blouse, then began to unfasten the buttons. Just then an intrusive aroma of pipe smoke mingled with Jessica's sweet breath. Jack whispered against her lips, "I think we have company..."

– 26 –

Alejandro's Story, Part 2

"Looks like me got here just in time, 'fore ya had a chance to butter 'er biscuit." Alejandro's rough voice cut through the hushed atmosphere of the cave like a foghorn.

Jack broke away from Jessica and glanced around. "I smell you and hear you, but I can't see you."

"Runnin' low on energy. M' time's near."

"Look, Jack. You can barely see him." Jessica pointed to a diminished Alejandro. His image wavered above the water, but his facial features were blurred. His body appeared wispy and fragmented, like a cloud formation.

"These caves be me ol' stompin' grounds."

"We thought you may have been here before," said Jack.

"Aye. Shelter from hurricanes. This ol' pirate's fadin' fast. We best git on wit' our business, 'afore it be too late."

"I thought you were gone for good when you disappeared last night," said Jessica. "I want to hear more about Rose Bodden."

"Before you start telling tales," said Jack, "what do you know about Ricky harassing Jessica?"

"Arr, he's like dog shit on me boots. Th' stink lingers long after ya step on 'im."

"You're aware Ricky's been stalking us?" Jessica raised an eyebrow.

"Aye."

"Why didn't you mention that earlier in the week?" Jack frowned, irritated with the ghost's cagey ways.

"Not supposed to meddle wit' th' living."

"What? Are you kidding me? All you've done this past week is meddle.

Jessica put her hand on Jack's arm. "Let's hear what Alejandro has to say. Don't want to waste the little time he has left flinging accusations."

"Smart woman," said the ghost. "Neither one of ya understands th' ways of th' dead, so listen up."

"Okay," said Jack, seating himself on a less-than-comfortable outcropping of rock. "I'm all ears."

"Ricky's been spyin' on ya with those things ya put up to yer eyes. Ya call 'em, what?"

"Binoculars?" asked Jessica.

"And th' night Jack made ya dinner? He accused me of stealin' yer ring, but Ricky was th' thievin' bilge rat."

Jack piped up, "I figured that out later."

"Left ya wit' a hint 'at night. Said ya had bigger problems than this old salt."

"Why didn't you just tell me about Ricky?" asked Jack.

"Spirits are supposed to let th' living figure out their own problems. Anyway, paid me a visit to Ricky that night and smashed his binoculars against th' building."

"Oh, my God! How did you do that?" Jessica asked.

"Takes a lot of me energy to move things. Ya numbskulls think ghosts can move stuff whenever they want, but 'ats not true. Anyway, after bustin' 'em up I warned Ricky to leave ya alone."

"In spite of your warning, he keeps popping up. First on the beach last night, and then cleaning the pool today." Jessica shook her head. "He's a problem."

"I leave tomorrow, Alejandro," said Jack. "So, if Ricky's as dangerous as I think he is, can you protect Jessica?"

"Me spirit's peterin' out. Not much this ol' salt can do. Besides, he likely won't be such a problem to ya now."

"Why not?" asked Jessica.

"Had 'im dancin' th' hempen jig last night."

"What the hell is that?"

"Did you assault him?" asked Jack.

"The less ya know about me and Ricky, th' better."

"I'm going to the police tomorrow morning with proof he's been tracking me." Jessica hesitated, lost in thought, then asked the ghost, "Why do you care that Ricky's stalking me? Why are you involved in our affairs if you're not supposed to be?"

"'Cuz of Rose Bodden. Made a promise to th' love of me life three hundred yar ago."

"What was the promise?"

The aroma of pipe smoke intensified. "Got time for th' rest of th' story?"

"Absolutely," said Jessica.

Jack shifted his weight on the uncomfortable rock and elevated his leg onto a nearby hunk of flat limestone, preparing himself for what promised to be a protracted story of Jessica's ancestors.

"Stayed on th' island after Rose nursed me to health. Had no ship, and nowhere to go. Lived in a raggedy thatched-roof house." The ghost puffed on his pipe, appearing to gather his thoughts. "One day, I saw her strollin' th' beach alone—called 'er name. Seemed glad to see me—laid 'er hand on me arm and asked how I was doin'. Her touch turned me heart soft as a jellyfish. I could tell she harbored a fondness for me, but I thought it born of loneliness. Not many people on th' island back then, and most of 'em were a rough, lawless bunch. Shipwrecked sailors, deserters from th' British Army, slaves, and pirates. She and her uncle were of the scant handful of folk wit' any means.

"After that, we fell into a pattern where we met on th' beach most days, away from th' pryin' eyes of her disapprovin' uncle.

Sometimes she brought Violet wit' her. That little girl loved to play in th' sand, always lookin' for th' perfect seashell."

Alejandro's image sharpened, revealing his face and most of his torso. He blinked and patted his chest. "Well, blow me down. Tellin' th' story's boostin' me energy. Comin' back to life." He pulled out his pipe and a tiny flame appeared in the bowl. "Been missin' me pipe."

"How does a ghost come back to life?" asked Jack.

"'Tis a figure of speech, ya prattlin' mutton-head. Stop askin' stupid questions."

"That's the Alejandro we know and love." Jessica laughed. "He's back, flinging insults."

The ghost glared at them. "As I was sayin', we got to be friendly, Rose and me. She loved me stories of th' sea and th' swashbucklin' ways of a pirate. Always teasin' me about buried treasure. I told her she was all th' treasure a pirate could want."

"That's so romantic," said Jessica.

"Romance is me middle name."

"Let's hear more about the buried treasure," Jack said through a smirk. "Know of any we can dig up?"

"Don't distract Alejandro," said Jessica. "I want to know about Rose."

"Aye. One October afternoon in 1717, a tropical storm swept through wit' no warnin'. Wind huffed hard enough to bend palm trees. I'd holed up in me little house, th' dirt floor wet wit' rain, and th' wind whistlin' through th' wattle and daub walls. There was a great poundin' on th' door, Rose's voice yellin' me name. I wrenched th' door open and pulled 'er in. She carried a small pot of turtle soup—liked to cook for me, ya know. Thought she could sneak out and get it to me before th' weather got so bad. But that storm was ragin'. Wasn't safe for man nor beast. We hunkered down together, and that's when our love affair began, wild 'n' unstoppable as a hurricane."

"You must really miss her." Jessica's forlorn tone revealed the depth her sympathy..

The ghost's eyes shone with unshed tears. "Aye. Won't be long now, and we'll be together again."

"Did you get married?" asked Jack.

"No. Remember, Rose's uncle hated me, so we had to meet on th' sly. After a few months, she got tired of sneakin' 'round and told her overbearin' uncle we were gettin' married no matter his attitude. Well, 'at set his head a-spinnin'. He screamed and ranted 'at no lawless, thievin' pirate scum was welcome in his family."

"What happened?" asked Jessica.

"Th' next day Rose missed our date, an' th' day after too. Mind ya, I didn't know she'd told her uncle what was what. So, I went lookin' for her. Got close to 'er home when one of their slaves, a woman that took care of th' house, intercepted me. Told me what happened between Rose and 'er uncle, then said 'at she had come down wit' a fever.

"The slave's name was Abby, and she loved Rose, as Rose was kindness itself, ya know. Told me Rose had been askin' fer me. Well, 'at was all this ol' salt needed to hear. I asked her to take me to Rose, and Abby led me to her bedroom. There she was, stretched out, lookin' yellow as butter, a bloodstained hanky in 'er hand. Me heart broke into a thousand pieces, fer I could tell she had yellow fever.

"Shoulda seen it comin'." Alejandro shook his head in a regretful way. "Days before Rose died, she said she was feelin' poorly. Had chills, didn't wanna eat—then she perked up some. But not long after, th' jaws of yellow fever clamped down on 'er. Couldn't help but wonder if her comin' to me in 'at storm made it worse."

"How awful," said Jessica. "You must've been devastated. What about Violet? Who was taking care of her with Rose so sick?"

"Abby took charge of Violet. The uncle, instead of bein' there for his family, he took to th' bottle. Ya see, he'd have to explain to his only brother why his only daughter died under his watch. He was an arsehole an' thought only of himself."

Jack asked, "So Rose died from yellow fever?"

"Aye. Her uncle tried to run me off like a mangy stray, but I threatened to skewer 'im wit' me cutlass. He gave up th' fight, and didn't darken th' door of Rose's bedroom again. I never left her side. She died in me arms a few days later—th' worst days of me life."

Alejandro's image flickered and dimmed. "Me energy's flaggin'. Don't know if I'll get through me story."

"Quickly, then. Tell us about the promise you made to Rose," said Jessica.

"Rose asked me to look after Violet; said th' little girl needed a strong man in 'er life on this brutal island. Since her uncle wasn't up to th' task, th' job fell to me. I loved Violet, and told Rose she'd never come to harm under me watchful eye.

"By then, Rose was dyin'. No savin' her from th' fever. I promised her I'd watch over not just Violet, but all th' women in her bloodline as long as I could. That includes ye too, Jessica. Yer me last project."

Jessica closed her eyes and took a deep breath. "Are you the ghost who saved my mother from that pot of boiling water?"

"Aye." Alejandro nodded and took a couple puffs of his pipe. "A man of me word—been keepin' an eye on all o' ya."

Jack glanced at Jessica, saw the tears on her face and squeezed her hand.

Jessica sniffed and asked the ghost, "What happened to Violet? Did she stay on this island?"

"Ah, little Violet was a spitfire. Looked just like her mama. I stayed close to 'er, and when she was about sixteen years old, she fell in love wit' Abby's son and married him. Her family was horrified she married a slave, but 'at was what life was like on this little island."

"So, um, when did you die?" asked Jack.

"About ten years later, when Violet had kids of 'er own. A couple of 'er daughters kept me busy. Hellions they were, runnin' wild around th' island."

"How did it happen?" asked Jessica.

"Downright embarrassin'. Died from a stab wound. Shoulda seen it comin' too. Playin' poker in a ramshackle tavern wit' a bunch of hornswagglin' sailors. They accused me of cheatin'. I called 'em a pack of lyin', scurvy-infested, bilge-drinkin' swabs. Turned and walked outta that ale-house. Barely got out th' door when a knife stuck me in th' back.

"I laid in a pool of me own blood. The proprietor took pity and sent someone to fetch Violet. She came a-runnin' and took me in, but no amount of nursin' could heal me. I died wit' 'er holdin' me hand."

"When did you become a ghost?" asked Jack.

"Well, 'twas so furious wit' th' chicken-shit way I died, 'at I refused to cross over. After all, I still had work to do. Had to protect Violet's girls."

"And now I'm the last of the line?" asked Jessica.

The pirate smiled just as a gust of wind blew through the cavern, taking his image with it.

"Oh no, Jack. He's gone!"

A chuckle hung on the restless air before Alejandro's disembodied voice whispered, "Me final task…ye're meant to be together."

Jack poured two glasses of Chablis and handed one to Jessica. After their cave experience, they'd decided to make a simple, home-cooked dinner of grilled chicken kebabs and a green salad. Tea light candles provided the only illumination on the screened-in patio where they relaxed. The rhythmic rumble of the surf served as the evening's music.

Jessica sipped the chilled wine, and frowned. "I don't want to take you to the airport tomorrow. I'll hate being apart from you."

"I hope so. I'd like to believe the other guys you've cycled on and off this island weren't so difficult to part with."

"Ha! You're a rare find, Jack. For you, I broke my rule of *not* getting involved with tourists. Please come back before April."

"I'll be back in a month, thanks to Caribbean Marine. And when I return, there won't be a ghost putting me through the paces."

"It'll be just us." Jessica smiled. "Well, and the boat dealer, since they're buying yachts from you."

"That's right."

Jessica hesitated, staring at Jack, absently twirling her wine glass.

"Go ahead," he said. "You look like something's on your mind."

"What do you think about Alejandro's last words?"

"That we're meant to be together?" asked Jack.

"Yes."

"I believe we *are* meant to be together." Jack hesitated, picking up on Jessica's serious vibe. "But, I was convinced of that without any ghostly prompting. My heart and my head agree. I love you, Jessica."

She gave a little smile. "It's easy to get carried away with romance. I've only known you for a few days ... a *wild* few days at that. But, I can't ignore the deep feelings I have for you ... and the strong physical attraction." Her eyes sparkled in the candlelight. "Maybe there really is some heavenly match-maker throwing us together."

"If that's true, then isn't it funny the matchmaker chose Alejandro to serve as the medium?" Jack laughed. "Just think, a ghostly pirate-Cupid, sent from the afterlife to bring us star-crossed mortals together. It boggles the mind."

"Whenever anyone asks us how we met, we'll have to leave out all the exciting parts. They'll never believe the real story."

"Now there's a good sign," said Jack.

"What?" asked Jessica.

"You used the word 'whenever.' You're talking about the future, and it seems I'm in it."

"Maybe we'll be telling our story for years to come. How 'bout that?"

Jack picked up Jessica's hand and kissed it. Imitating Alejandro's voice, he whispered, "Ya hit me like a bolt of lightnin', and then ya stole me heart."

– 27 –

Leaving on a Jet Plane

Jack transferred the snoozing Carrots from his packed suitcase to the bed, realizing cat hair was the only souvenir he was taking home with him. There'd been no time for shopping. He zipped his suitcase shut, wheeled it into the kitchen, and poured himself a cup of coffee.

Jessica left early that morning to attend a business meeting, so he wandered out onto the screened patio, alone with his thoughts. Last night's memories pelted him from all directions. He contemplated the ghost's final words. *If we're truly meant to be together, how would it play out? Will she be willing to live in Michigan? Can I replace my career on a small Caribbean island?* Although he produced a sizable income, his job wasn't a dream job. He'd be open to a change if the right opportunity came along, and maybe that'd be on Cayman Island.

He breathed in, savoring the humid sea air. The baby-blue sky and brilliant sunshine would soon be replaced by the blah of a typical Michigan winterscape. His mind's eye conjured up a scene resembling a washed-out black-and-white photo—streets covered with dirty, slushy snow, imposing mountains of the stuff piled up in parking lots. Top it off with a sky crammed with thick, gray clouds. He couldn't picture Jessica in such a drab setting. He often cursed the dreary, sunless weather that dominated Michigan for five months of the year, but if he moved to this little island, would he just be trading snow for hurricanes?

"Hey, you." Jessica's voice broke into his ruminations.

Before he could turn around, she wrapped her arms around his waist. "I've been watching you for the last couple minutes. Looked like you were deep in thought."

"I was. Thinking about you and this beautiful place. Don't want to leave."

"Then don't."

"Have to. Duty calls."

"Hurry back."

"You can count on it." He turned to face Jessica and kissed her, his hands tracing her hips and waist. He cupped her breasts. "I wonder how these will look on Skype?"

"They'll look magnificent." She grinned and patted him below the belt. "And, what about this?"

"Oh, it'll fill up your laptop's screen."

"Really? I can't wait to see that."

"Hmm. What about spying eyes on the internet? Someone hacking into Skype? Sounds risky to me."

"See what I mean about you being a bit buttoned-down?" Jessica pinched his rear.

"Considering this bizarre week, I can probably be talked into anything, including Skype sex."

"Before I forget, do you have the Find My Friends app on your phone?" asked Jessica.

"No. Never heard of it."

"I can see where you are, and vice-versa. Since we're going to be apart for a while, it'd be another fun way to stay in touch."

"Sounds like a stalker app Ricky would have on his phone."

"It takes two people to use the app." Jessica rolled her eyes. "I'm betting no one's interested in keeping track of Ricky. You can shut it off anytime you want. Like, if you don't want me to know you've shown up at my condo for a surprise visit."

"Okay, I'll load the app, but I'm more interested in

exploring the surprise visit." He held her chin and caressed her cheek with his thumb. "Please tell me I'll "find" you at the police station shortly after you drop me off at the airport?"

"You will. I have the tracker in my purse to show the police. I'm counting on Ricky backing off when he's served with a restraining order."

"Let's hope so. He needs to go away."

Jack pulled Jessica into an embrace and breathed in her scent. "I'm really going to miss you," he said, amazed at how profoundly he dreaded their coming time apart.

"I can't see you for a whole month. Seems like an eternity."

"I'm gonna force myself to buckle down and work, although the overwhelming temptation will be to stare out the window and think of you in this tropical paradise."

Jessica whispered in his ear, "And I can dream of you looking all sexy in low-slung jeans and a cozy flannel shirt."

He held her closer. "As long as we're fantasizing, have you fallen in love with me yet? I keep thinking of Alejandro's parting words."

"That's all I can think about, Jack. During your next visit, there won't be any distractions. It'll be all about us. We'll see how things go."

"No more ghosts and cruise ship tours?"

"Nope. Just you, me, the beach and my bed."

"Naughty girl."

"It's time for this naughty girl to take you to the airport. Are you all packed and ready to go?"

"I suppose." Jack heaved a sigh. He grabbed his suitcase and opened the door. The short walk to the car was enough to make him realize how out of place his jeans were in the tropical weather. They felt hot and heavy on his legs, but he'd need them where he was headed. They got into Jessica's car, and he cranked the air conditioning.

Minutes later, Jessica turned into the airport's parking lot and grabbed a ticket from the machine.

"Hey, you don't have to park. Just slow down by the entrance and I'll jump out."

"Oh, stop it. I'm giving you a proper send-off. Besides, you can't deprive me of one last kiss."

Jessica zipped into an empty spot and shut off the engine. Jack grabbed her hand and squeezed it. "I want you to know you're amazing, and I love you."

Jessica leaned across the console and kissed him. "I'm already counting the days."

"As much as I hate it," said Jack, "let's do this." Jessica popped the trunk, and Jack retrieved his suitcase.

Chickens roamed around the landscaping surrounding the airport entrance, pecking at the sparse grass. The bright red combs on top of their heads resembled sassy hats that complimented their multi-colored plumage. A few brave ones dodged the steady stream of human feet and roller bags to peck at cracks in the sidewalk. "I'll bet you don't see free-range poultry at the airport in Grand Rapids, do you?" Jessica grinned.

"Nope. Just one more charming feature of Grand Cayman Island. Does anyone feed these birds?" Jack dodged a cinnamon-colored hen, her sights set on some cracker crumbs.

"No. They're feral and self-supporting. People either love 'em or hate 'em."

Jack opened the door to the airport. The conditioned air was only slightly cooler than outside. Long lines snaked around airline kiosks and counters. Loud blasts from the public address system squawked redundant security reminders. He hoped it'd be quieter in the waiting areas.

"I guess this is it. All carry-on luggage, so no long check-in lines for me." He stared at Jessica, taking in every detail, from her ponytail secured by a pink satin ribbon to her small feet in white, strappy sandals.

Jessica pressed against him and whispered, "Think about me every day. Call me. Text me. Email me. Skype me. Send me naughty pictures. I want it all."

"Then you shall have it all." He kissed her one last time, then made his way to the security line.

Jessica turned away and headed for the parking lot. Now alone, she felt eager to sort out the mad scramble of emotions occupying her head and heart. She'd fallen for Jack, but the ghost's pronouncement that they were meant to be together was a bit unsettling. Was her free will being usurped? A yellow caution light blinked in her head. One poor relationship choice was enough for a lifetime.

She clutched her handbag. Feeling the outline of the tracking device made her frown and think about Ricky planting it on her car. Talk about bad decisions. Marrying him was undoubtedly the worst mistake of her life. Her next stop would be the police station. She'd decided a restraining order was necessary, though she wondered if Ricky might be provoked by such a move. Would he man up and respect her and the law? Or, would he continue to indulge in his juvenile stalking behavior?

She opened the car door, situated herself behind the wheel, and started the engine. A tap on the passenger's side window caught her attention.

"Hey, Jessie. Missing something?" A smiling Ricky waggled her cell phone.

Jessica's heart thudded. She frowned and whispered, "Fuck," cracking the passenger's window just wide enough for Ricky to slide the phone in. "I'm not even going to ask how you got my phone. Slip it through the window."

"You know, you really should lock your car, Jessie." Ricky coughed, cleared his throat and croaked, "And never leave your phone in the cup holder on such a hot day. Heat's very bad for electronics."

"Stop screwing around, and give me the phone. I've gotta go to work."

"Always so dutiful and dedicated, aren't you? Tell me, does Jack take a back seat to your work like I did? Or does he enjoy a higher status than ol' fuckin' Ricky?"

"Give me my phone."

Ricky arranged his features into a sincere look. "I'll give you your phone if you let me talk to you for just a few minutes. In the car. It's hotter than hell out here."

"You can talk to me through the window."

"No, I can't. It's about my mom, Jessie." He cleared his throat again, turned his head away and bit his lower lip. "She's been diagnosed with cancer."

Jessica closed her eyes as the bad news sunk in. For all of Ricky's faults, he had a fabulous mother, Grace, and she and Jessica had been very close. Since the divorce, they'd tried to have lunch with some regularity, but those get-togethers became less frequent as time passed.

"That's awful." She shook her head and sighed. "I don't have much time; five minutes."

She popped the locks, and Ricky got into the passenger seat. She held out her hand. "Okay. Phone, please, and then tell me about Grace."

"You mean this phone?" He taunted her with it, holding it just out of her reach.

"Hand it over." She lunged for it, but Ricky opened the window and tossed it into a shrub at the edge of the parking lot. He then pulled a gun from the waistband of his shorts.

He pointed it at Jessica, low and out of sight. "Let's roll. I'll tell you where to go."

Jessica fought down her panic and took a deep breath. *Dear God, help me out of this one. Help me keep a clear head.*

She glared at Ricky. "Shall I assume Grace doesn't have cancer?"

"Ding! Ding! Ding! Ding! You always were the smart one, weren't you?"

– 28 –

Flightus Interruptus

A Tortuga rum cake display in front of the duty-free store caught Jack's eye. The packaging logo featured a pirate-type ship. *Wonder if Alejandro is with Rose now, all happy together in the hereafter? I hope so.*

"Would you like to try a sample?" asked a young woman holding a tray of bite-sized rum cake pieces.

"Sure." He popped one in his mouth. Rummy, rich and buttery. "Delicious. I'll take two cakes."

Jack felt grateful for the last-minute shopping opportunity. His administrative assistant covered for him while he was away; the least he could do was come back with a token of thanks. Only a week away from the office, but it felt like a year. Although pleased with his success at Caribbean Marine, he realized he had to knuckle down when he returned to Michigan. For now, all he wanted to do was replay the past week in his mind.

He found a seat in the crowded waiting area, pulled out his phone, and loaded Find My Friends, curious how the thing worked. He opened the app, and a little map appeared showing a green pulsing dot indicating Jessica's location. Jack frowned. *Still at the airport.* He'd left her over half an hour ago. *Should be at the police station. Strange. I'll call her.*

Jack punched the numbers. The phone rang several times before going to voicemail. He left a message. "Hey, there. Just trying out the Find My Friends app, and saw you're still at the airport. Give me a call and let me know what's up."

He checked email and the news until the overhead speaker blasted an announcement, at an ear-bleeding decibel, indicating his flight was boarding. He joined the line forming at the gate. *Haven't heard from Jessica.* He frowned. *Don't be a worry-wart. She's probably tied up on a business call.*

Jack rechecked the app. The pulsing green dot hadn't moved. He called again, and got the same results. *Maybe the app isn't working. I'll try her office number.* He thumbed through his contacts, but before he found what he was looking for the faintest whiff of pipe smoke caught his attention.

He glanced around, trying to spot any sign of Alejandro, but saw nothing. His skin prickled, and his concern for Jessica escalated. The line moved as people began boarding the plane. Another blast of pipe smoke wafted by; this time, the aroma was so intense the woman in front of him turned around. "Is someone smoking a pipe?"

Jack ignored her. *Alejandro's trying to get my attention. Is Jessica in trouble? No point just standing here wondering.* He left the boarding area and headed to the immigration counters, the only thing separating the main airport from the departure gates. Not an agent in sight, either to stop him or help him. He hurried to the main doors, exited, made a beeline for the parking lot, and saw that Jessica's spot was empty. He looked around the small lot, her little Prius nowhere to be seen.

He tapped her number and heard a faint chime he recognized as her ringtone. Walking in the direction of the sound, he stopped by a row of scabby bushes at the edge of the parking lot. He found Jessica's phone, face-down in the dirt, stuck in a tangle of woody branches.

Jack fished the phone out of the overgrown plant. Anger

swept through him. "Message received, Alejandro. Jessica's in danger. That bastard Ricky's the cause, isn't he?"

A curl of pipe smoke whirled in the breeze, confirming his suspicions.

Traffic crawled along at twenty-five miles per hour on the Esterly Tibbetts Highway, but Jessica's mind clocked a hundred miles a minute. *As slow as this traffic is, I could probably jump out.* But all she saw was the gun. Fear made her hot and sweaty. Panic simmered beneath her outward calm. *Does Ricky want to scare me, or harm me?* She knew he was emotionally unhinged, and could easily imagine him killing her before turning the gun on himself.

"Ricky, where did you get that gun?"

"I found it."

"Bullshit. Stop pointing it at me."

"Stop telling me what to do. Just keep driving. A few more miles." He coughed and cleared his throat.

"What's wrong with your voice?"

"Don't play dumb with me."

"I don't know what you're talking about. Where the hell are we going?"

"You'll see."

He seemed eerily calm, which worried Jessica. Like he'd made up his mind about how things would play out, and was okay with it.

"Turn left here."

Jessica turned east, heading away from Georgetown and the Seven Mile Beach area. "We're going to Bodden Town?"

"Stop asking questions."

Jessica shook her head, irritated by Ricky's terse answers.

After a couple more miles, Ricky rasped, "Turn right here."

She headed down a narrow two-track. "We're going to our old beach spot?"

"Thought it'd help get you in the proper frame of mind."

"For what?" She took a deep breath. *Just great. A trip down literal memory lane.*

"Park here."

Jessica pulled the car under a palm tree. To her right sat the old shuttered inn the locals believed to be haunted by a pirate ghost. Alejandro had admitted he was that ghost. *Wish you were here now, buddy. I could use your help.*

The beach surrounding the inn was primo—tucked back in a little cove, partially concealed by a stand of palm trees, within walking distance of Spotts Public Beach. Her romance with Ricky began at this popular secluded hangout, in her junior year.

"You're quiet, Jess. I know you're thinking of old times—better times." He nudged her leg with the snubnose barrel of the gun. "We can get those back if you just hear me out."

"Ricky, we're divorced. You've kidnapped me. I have nothing to say to you. Especially when you have a gun and are *touching* me with it."

"I'd touch you with more than a gun, if you'd let me."

That did it. Her anger spilled over like hot lava. She screamed, "You worthless piece of shit! Let's end this right now. Get the fuck out of my car."

Ricky's eyes narrowed as he moved the gun up to her face. He croaked out his words. "I tried to be nice, but if this is…" He coughed.

"What the fuck's the matter with you?"

With his free hand he reached in his shirt pocket and pulled out a chicken foot talisman, black feathers were tied to the foot with twine, red and black beads dangling from one of the digits. Sneering, Ricky waved the grotesque thing in her face.

"Like you don't know, you devious, evil whore. Your pet ghost almost strangled me to death. Let's see if he comes to your rescue now."

"What?" She reared back in revulsion. "Have you lost your goddamn mind?"

Ricky dropped the talisman, grabbed Jessica's arm and twisted it.

"Let go of me!" She yanked her arm from Ricky's grasp, the gun still aimed at her head.

The car suddenly filled with the aroma of roses. *What? Roses? Rose…Rose Bodden!* That was all the encouragement she needed.

"Devious? You want devious? I'll show you devious." She scooped up the handbag by her feet and plunged her hand inside, fishing around for the tracking device, never taking her eyes off Ricky. She found it right next to the canister of pepper spray.

She hurled the tracking device at Ricky's face, leaving a bloody divot on his forehead. "How about that, you sick bastard? How dare you stalk me?"

"Crazy bitch!" Ricky put his hands up in defense and the gun went off, blasting a hole in the roof of the car. The deafening explosion pushed Jessica's fear into the red zone. *He's gonna kill me!*

She groped for the pepper spray, pulled it from her purse and fired it into Ricky's face. He bellowed and dropped the gun, rubbing his eyes while groping for the door handle. As she gave him another blast, his door flew open and he bailed into the sand, coughing and gagging.

Residual pepper spray lingered in the car. Jessica's eyes burned and watered, impairing her vision. She jammed the car into reverse and cut the wheel. The passenger door swung wildly before slamming shut. She felt the bump before she heard the hair-raising scream. A quick, blurry look over her shoulder confirmed she'd run over Ricky.

Panicked, she threw the car into drive and careened down the sandy two-track, tearing off a side mirror on a palm tree. She wiped her eyes with the back of her hand, trying to clear her vision—an instant before ramming into a fire hydrant. The airbag deployed with a loud *bang!* Stunned, tears coursing down her cheeks, she began to shake.

Jessica scrambled from the car to stare at the mangled left front wheel. Her legs wobbled, and she collapsed on the sidewalk, sobbing.

– 29 –

Jack's Turn

Jack slipped Jessica's phone into his backpack, nabbing the first taxi in the line-up at the curb. He tossed his suitcase in the back seat and got in front with the driver. "Please take me to the nearest police station."

"That'd be Bodden Town, about twenty minutes and forty dollars. That okay?

"Fine."

The driver pulled out into the congested traffic. "Just arriving?"

"No. Been here for about a week."

The man nodded. "Most people who get a cab at the airport are going to a hotel or condo. Not many need a ride to the police station."

Jack was aware of the driver's attempt to ferret out his story. He snuck a glance at the cabbie—older, pleasant demeanor. *What the hell? I'm in uncharted waters. Could use a friend.*

"I think my girlfriend's in trouble. That's why I need the police."

"What kind of trouble?" The driver frowned.

"She may have been forced to go somewhere with her ex-husband. As in kidnapped."

"Oh no. Was she traveling with you?"

"No. She lives here, a native Caymanian. Manages the Sandy Beach Resort."

"You mean Jessica Banks?"

"Yes. You know her?"

"Sure do. Refers a lot of her guests to our cab company. What makes you think she's been kidnapped?"

"Her ex has been stalking her. Can't seem to get it through his thick head that she's done with him. He put a GPS tracker on her car—we also had a run-in with him on the beach."

"You're doing the right thing going to the police. Jessica's a fine young woman. Hate to think of her in a bad situation. By the way, I'm Dexter."

"I'm Jack. Nice to meet you, Dexter."

Jack made an effort to think clearly, but all he could picture was Jessica in Ricky's clutches, him doing God-knows-what to her. It felt like the taxi was turtle-crawling down the street, which stressed him to the point of snapping.

Some distance ahead, a car jutting out into the street caught Jack's eye. He leaned forward, squinting. *Is that Jessica's car?*

"Dexter, see that up ahead?"

"The car that looks like it's hung up on a fire hydrant?"

"Yup. Pull over. Could be Jessica."

Dexter eased his taxi to the shoulder. Jack jumped out and ran to the damaged Prius. He found Jessica sitting on the side-walk, knees pulled tight to her chest, head down, and sobbing.

His heart clutched. "Jessica!"

She looked up, an expression of disbelief on her reddened, tear-streaked face. "How did you find me?"

"Are you hurt? Can you stand?"

Jack helped her to her feet and gathered her in his arms. "Oh my God. Are you okay?"

"I'm *not* okay." Her sobbing intensified. "I… I killed Ricky."

"What?!" A bolt of fear shot through Jack. He took a deep

breath to calm himself, smoothing Jessica's hair away from her face. "How did it happen?"

"I backed over him— trying to get away. It was an accident."

Jack felt worried, but he tried to keep his voice low and calm. "Where is he now?"

Jessica pointed down the two-track. "Back there."

"Walking distance?"

She nodded, a stunned look on her face.

"You sit in the cab with Dexter, and I'll walk back there. Okay?"

She shook her head. "No. Don't go. Stay with me."

Jack led her to the taxi and helped her into the passenger's seat. "Call the police, Dexter. Tell them we need an ambulance. Look after Jessica for me."

"Sure thing." Dexter picked up his cell phone.

"Jack, he had a gun. He would've killed me..."

"You're safe here, Jessica. The police will be along. Tell them you were kidnapped at gunpoint. We'll sort this out. You did nothing wrong. Remember, I love you."

Hyper-alert, he headed down the dirt track. *Have to find Ricky. How does she know for sure she killed the jackass?* If Ricky were dead, there was nothing to fear—but, if alive, Jack would have a gun-wielding nut-job on his hands. As much as the idea of Ricky in an early grave appealed to him, the legal ramifications were unappealing. He couldn't stand the thought of Jessica being hauled off in handcuffs because of that worthless asshole.

Jack saw a lump of something in the distance. *Oh shit. Maybe she did kill him.* He walked closer. The lump finally stirred and moaned. *Alive, but not well.* He breathed deeply, trying to calm his banging heart. *Where's that gun?*

He slipped behind a palm tree and watched. Ricky tried to sit up but fell back, gasping. His left leg appeared useless.

He groaned and cursed, lying supine on the sand. *No sign of a gun.*

Jack called out, "Do you need help?"

"Fuck yes! My leg's broken."

He stepped from behind the tree and approached Ricky. "You don't look so good."

Ricky stared at Jack. Recognition flickered in his swollen eyes. "Oh, it's you. You gotta help me, man. Call an ambulance."

"I'd rather call a hearse for your sorry ass. Where's your gun, big man?"

"Don't have one." He showed his hands, palms up. "Come on. My leg's broken." He pointed to a bloody bulge on his thigh.

"Well, look at that. Your bone's poking through the skin. Maybe if I step on it, the bone will snap back into place. Think what you'll save in medical bills."

Jack nudged the broken leg with his foot. Ricky howled and tried to grab Jack, who dodged the clumsy attempt.

"You sick prick," croaked Ricky. "Your whore did this to me..."

"Did you say whore?" Anger surged through Jack like a lightning strike. He gave the injured leg a swift kick.

"Stop! Stop!" Ricky breathed through clenched teeth, his face contorted with pain, sweat glistening on his forehead.

"Now, who's a whore, Ricky?"

"No one," he said, panting. "Nobody's a whore."

"That's better. Lucky for you, we've already called an ambulance... and the police."

Ricky closed his eyes. "Didn't want to hurt Jessica... only wanted to talk to her."

"So you kidnapped her? You've got all the smooth moves, man. And you had a gun? Kidnapping at gunpoint's a serious offense, Ricky. I wonder what it's like doing time in a Caymanian jail? Probably no air conditioning."

Ricky sobbed, tears and snot streaming down his puffy face. He whispered, "Don't you get it? I love her."

Jack turned his back on the pathetic heap on the ground. The distant wail of sirens sounded, spurring him down the track toward Jessica.

– 30 –

Debriefing

Carrots jumped up on Jessica's lap, curled up into a tight ball and closed his eyes. Occasionally, his whiskers and tail twitched, as if to let her know he was merely dozing and could spring into action in the blink of a cat's eye. She stroked his soft fur, tears slipping unheeded down her cheeks.

Jack watched from the kitchen, surprised at the cat's intuition. The minute Jessica entered the condo Carrots pounced into caregiver mode. Appearing to sense her anguish, he wound around her legs and meowed until she picked him up. As she cried into his fur he absorbed her stress and misery like a sponge, putting his paw on her cheek for comfort.

Today had been as shitty as a day could possibly be. Kidnapping, gunshots, accidents, cops, and an unhealthy dose of Ricky. To knock the edge off, Jack filled two glasses with ice, a generous portion of local rum, and a splash of orange juice. He handed one of the cocktails to Jessica, kissed her cheek, and sat next to her on the sofa.

"Drink up. Dr. Jack's orders."

Jessica smiled, but her watery eyes looked sad. "You came to my rescue."

"You saved yourself, Jessica. You figured a way out and took it. No small thing, considering the stress you were under."

"Thanks to pepper spray. The second time I've used it this week."

"Yeah, the drunk guy on the beach took a hit too, didn't he?"

Jessica nodded. Fresh tears streamed down her face. "This isn't me, you know."

"What do you mean?" He took her hand.

"I've never been a victim like this."

"Ricky ambushed you. It's not your fault."

"I fell for his story about his mother having cancer."

"He's a conniving fuck, and worked you like only a conniving fuck can. This is all on Ricky. And now look where he is. In the hospital, under guard."

"Will he go to jail?"

"Sergeant Andrews told me a kidnapping sentence guarantees a minimum of fourteen years in jail—likely more because of the gun."

"I can't believe he actually pulled a gun on me. I wonder where he got it? Guns aren't that easy to come by here."

"Who knows? That's for Sergeant Andrews to figure out."

Jessica nodded. "God*damn* Ricky." She turned and faced Jack, her eyes narrowing, mouth twisted with rage. "How dare that worthless fuck make me a victim? When I parked the car, I lost it... threw the tracking device at his face. Then the blast of the gun... I thought he was going to kill me. I, I shot him with pepper spray. He fell out of the car... my only chance to escape. So I took off. I'll never forget the feel of running over him... the bumps, his screams. Now I get to live with those nightmares."

"I hate that. At the same time, remember you were justified—that you feared for your life. Ricky's lucky only his leg got broken. He had it coming, Jessica. Holding someone at gunpoint... c'mon."

Jessica gave him a grateful look. "He didn't think I'd fight back. Assumed I wouldn't."

"He underestimated you." Jack kissed her and wiped away her tears. "I was concerned how the police would handle it. Would they haul you away? Charge you with a hit-and-run? I've heard stories of police corruption on Jamaica. Didn't know if I'd have to bribe anyone to keep you safe, or out of jail."

Jessica shrugged. "Cayman's not a third world country."

"I know that now. Where else would you see this motto on a police car: 'We Care, We Listen, We Act?'"

"I always thought they put that on the police cars for the tourists' benefit." Jessica gave a wry smile.

Jack smiled back, even as he stared into the distance.

Jessica raised her eyebrows. "What?"

"When you told me you'd killed Ricky, I took off to find him. When I did, I realized he only had a broken leg; a relief, but it also pissed me off. It was like okay, he's alive, so now I want to kill him. You know how people say they want just five minutes alone with someone that's done them wrong?"

Jessica nodded. "Yes."

"Well, I taunted Ricky, who was lying on the ground, helpless. He called me a sick prick, and you a whore. I snapped and kicked his broken leg as hard as I could." Jack heaved a sigh and closed his eyes. "He almost passed out, but I kept yelling at him until he took his words back." He opened his eyes and stared at Jessica. "What the hell does that make me?"

"You were provoked." She frowned, disgust showing on her face. "We've been harassed and stalked by Ricky all week. It's only natural we'd both have some pent-up aggression."

"I wanted to make him pay for what he did to you. What would a psychologist say about that? I failed to protect you, so I doled out punishment instead?"

"Jack, we could psychoanalyze all day, but we're human, and sometimes we act out—especially under stress. I'm sick of thinking about today... I just want to move on, though it'll probably hang with me for a while."

Jessica removed Carrots from her lap and placed him on the floor. He stretched and sauntered over to his food bowl, his role as support cat suspended for a while.

Jack stood and held out his hands. "Wanna go outside? Maybe sit on the beach?"

"Sure."

He helped her up, drew her into an embrace, and whispered, "Remember, I love you. You'll be fine."

Jack refreshed their drinks, and they headed for the beach. He led her to a shady spot where they sat quietly for a little while. He glanced at Jessica. Her eyes were closed, her body still.

As if she felt his gaze, Jessica put her hand on Jack's arm. "Any ghostly contact from Alejandro today?"

"Yeah. Just when I thought he was gone for good. In fact, it was the aroma of his pipe smoke that alerted me to your danger."

"Tell me about it."

"The Find My Friends app showed you were still at the airport, long after you should've been on your way to the police station. I thought maybe the app wasn't working, but I couldn't ignore the sense that something wasn't right. I interpreted smelling pipe smoke at the boarding gate as a message from Alejandro that you needed help. I ran to the parking lot and discovered your phone."

"So, Alejandro's still out there somewhere," said Jessica, "apparently not too far away, watching over us. They should rename the app Find My Friend's *Phone*."

"Agreed. I'm grateful our friendly pirate intervened. I wonder if we'll ever see him again."

"I kind of miss him. Guess what? I had my own brush with the beyond today." Jessica smiled and sipped her drink.

"Really? Alejandro?"

"No. Rose Bodden. Just before I sprayed Ricky, the car

filled with the fragrance of roses. I think she was sending me the strength—the final push—I needed to escape from Ricky."

"Like it or not, we're linked to these souls." Jack reached over and cupped her chin, trailing his thumb over the little dimple. "I think Alejandro was right—we're meant to be together. Do you see that now?"

"Yes. I love you, Jack." She leaned in and kissed him.

I love you. The three most significant words in life. Jack's heart responded with a series of happy thuds, even as a caution light blinked from the sidelines. *Does she really mean it?*

"Jessica, I've dreamed of this moment, but I need to know it's really you talking, and not just a reaction to all the drama."

"I wanted to tell you when we said good-bye this morning, but the airport was too busy and noisy... not exactly a romantic setting. I just wanted the moment to be right. So, here we are. Not as romantic as I'd like, but will it do?" Jessica put her hand to Jack's cheek.

He grinned and took her hand. "This day just went from being the worst to the best day of my life. I love you so much."

"I've never experienced the kind of tenderness and care you gave me when you showed up at the accident scene." Jessica's eyes welled up with tears. "I trust you with my heart, Jack, and I need you."

"So, my sweet, where do we go from here?"

"How about my bedroom? I could use a little TLC."

– 31 –

Sexual Healing

Something happened on the stroll back from the beach, but Jack wasn't sure what. Jessica had grown quiet, but he chalked it up to weariness from the day. He understood why she needed a little TLC. After a day of all sharp edges, he wanted to comfort her any way he could. But when they crossed the threshold into the condo, she locked the door, rushed at him, grabbed his shirt up with her fists, and backed him against the kitchen wall. Surprised by her aggressive move, he cupped her chin and studied her face, looking for clues. She returned his stare with narrowed eyes, a determined set to her chin. *Angry? Aroused?* He was part of the scene, but didn't know his role.

"Are you okay?" He rested his hands on her hips. She put her index finger to his lips, shushing him, and pressed against him, moving just so, never breaking eye contact.

She whispered, "Close your eyes."

He did. Her hands flattened on his chest, and she began tugging and pulling at his shirt until his chest was bare. Licking and nipping, her mouth left a damp trail from his neck to his shoulder. He reached out to pull her closer, but she stopped him with a firm "no", putting his hands at his sides.

When her soft, hot mouth covered his, he groaned and sank into the swirl of sensations. She kissed him for a long while, slow and deliberate, finally dancing her tongue along his lower lip. Her desire to control excited him. She directed the scene.

Unable to remain passive, Jack shifted his stance and pushed his erection into her hip. Jessica quickly removed her top and bra, pressing her naked chest to his. Heat rolled off her fevered body. Instinct moved his hands up her sides, yearning to touch her soft breasts. She batted his hands away, undid his buckle, and dragged down the zipper of his pants. Her hand, so hot, gripped his shaft and stroked him; he shuddered, calling on all his reserves to keep it together.

They stumbled into the bedroom. Jack unbuttoned her skirt. She kicked it aside and stood before him, naked, wild as sin. She then sank to the floor and took him into her mouth. He braced himself against the wall—afraid he might burst. Her need was unrestrained... wanton. He feared the scene would end too fast, so he pulled her to her feet. Her stare was unsettling, her dark eyes blazing with arousal.

"Fuck me, Jack."

So he did.

– 32 –

Back to Reality

The aroma of freshly brewed coffee awakened Jack before the alarm. He reached for Jessica on the other side of the bed, but felt only the still-warm sheets. Bleary-eyed, he checked the time. Seven o'clock. He heaved a sigh. Sleep had eluded him for most of the night. His mind had refused to power down, and he'd relived the day's drama and the evening's sexual frenzy in one long, continuous loop.

"Hey, lover boy. Rise and shine." Jessica swooped into the room, placing a steaming cup of coffee on the bedside stand. Her white terry cloth robe hung open, and he caught a whiff of scented soap.

He hooked his arm around her waist and pulled her on top of him. "Hey, yourself. Thanks for the coffee. You spoil me."

"Least I could do after the rough treatment I doled out last night." She grinned and kissed his nose.

"I'm a tough guy. I can take it." He slid his hands underneath her robe and caressed her bare skin. "How are *you*?"

"I'm okay. Slept like the dead... thanks to you."

"Sexual exhaustion?" He kissed her neck.

"More like sexual healing. How 'bout you?"

"Well, more like a nice nap. Maybe got in two hours toward morning. Kept thinking about how I don't wanna leave today."

“Then don’t.” She traced her finger along his jawline. “I love you, and I need you here with me.”

“You told me you loved me yesterday. For the first time.”

“Mm-hmm.” She nodded.

“It changed everything. I felt this seismic shift…full speed ahead, no turning back.”

“It’s real love, Jack. The forever kind.”

“I’ll be back in a month. Seems so far away…”

Jessica whispered, “Live in the now.” She slipped the robe from her shoulders. “How ‘bout one for the road?”

The taxi rolled to a stop at the airport entrance. Jack and Jessica exchanged glances.

“Kinda weird, isn’t it?” asked Jack.

“Yeah. Returning to the scene of the crime…literally.” Jessica shuddered.

“No crimes today. I promise.”

They got out of the taxi. Jack removed his roller bag from the trunk and told the driver to wait for Jessica. The same chickens he’d seen yesterday were busy pecking in the scabby grass—until a little kid dropped his bag of Cheetos. A mad scramble ensued as several Attila the Hens squawked and pecked at the orange treats.

“These chickens crack me up.” Jack grinned.

“Entertaining, aren’t they?” Jessica winked. “Just another reason to come back.”

“Did I need another reason?”

“I sensed you were waffling.”

“Me? Never.” Jack gathered her into a hug and whispered, “This is it, pretty girl. I’ve gotta go. Before I land in Grand Rapids, I’ll be dreaming of my return trip. Chickens and all.”

A couple tears trickled down her face. "I love you so much. I miss you already. A month is too long."

"Love you too. The taxi's waiting, and I see the security line's jamming up. Good-bye, sweetie. I'll text you when I land."

Jessica headed for the exit, blowing him a kiss as she pushed through the doors to the outside.

A dull ache pulsed in the back of Jack's head, and his stomach churned. He frowned. *Stress? Love sick? Flu?* His body seemed to be reacting to the turmoil of the entire week. Sweat formed on his forehead as the tight serpentine security line inched along. The packed room was noisy and hot—security personnel barked out orders, while the air conditioning dripped condensation and expelled tepid air.

Fifteen minutes later, he was in the departure bullpen, waiting to board. The air conditioning felt cooler here, but his head still throbbed. *Can't wait a month.* They'd planned his return trip around their business schedules. Now that their relationship had jumped to the next level, he couldn't accept being apart from her for that long.

He touched the airline's app on his phone and searched for flights. One seat was left on a direct flight from Detroit to Grand Cayman in just two weeks. On impulse, he jumped at the opportunity and secured the reservation. He smiled. The throbbing in his head waned.

Jack took one last look at the lapis blue of the Caribbean as the plane rose above the clouds. Exhaustion covered him like a flannel blanket. Grateful nobody sat next to him, Jack stretched his legs across the empty seat. He tried to fall asleep, but his mind raced.

Jessica was his present and future. *But how does that match up with the other parts of my life?* He mulled over his job. He made good money and enjoyed the success, but it didn't define him. *And what about friends and family?* They were just a plane ride away. It wouldn't be the first time a man moved abroad to be with the woman he loved.

Jack closed his eyes and finally nodded off.

"Hey, matey. Move yer legs."

Jack, clinging to sleep, reluctantly moved his legs and repositioned his head to lean against the window.

"Psst." Annoyed with another intrusion, Jack opened just one eye. Alejandro's face filled his line of vision.

"What are you doing here?" mumbled Jack. "You crossed over. Let me sleep." He tried to push the ghost away. Instead of his hand passing through thin air, he touched human flesh. "Wait, are you real now?" His sleep-fogged brain struggled to keep up.

"Aye." The pirate took the seat next to Jack and whisper-shouted, "What's a scalawaggin' pirate have to do for a bit o' rum 'round here?"

Jack blinked and pointed to the overhead controls. "Push the red button."

Alejandro repeatedly jabbed the button. "Where's me rum?"

"Don't be so impatient. The flight attendant will come by. Be polite. None of your usual snarky comments."

The pirate guffawed. "Even in your dream state, yer barkin' out orders."

"Who's dreaming? I'm awake now, thanks to your inconsiderate ass."

"Ye ain't awake, ya clueless nitwit."

The flight attendant came by. She gave Alejandro an appraising look. "Nice outfit. What can I do for you?"

"Rum, me sweet. 'At's all a pirate ever needs. Well, that an' a lusty wench."

She narrowed her eyes and produced a forced smile. "Is Bacardi okay?"

"That th' wench's name?" Alejandro waggled his eyebrows. "Exotic."

"No, ya daft mongrel," interrupted Jack, "that's the brand name of the rum. Thank you, ma'am, Bacardi will be fine. I'll take one too… with a Coke."

"So now yer drinkin' wit' me?"

Jack glanced at his watch. "Got another two hours in the air, might as well make them count." He studied the pirate, his features more pronounced in the flesh-and-blood version. "You know, you don't look as old in real life as you did as a ghost."

"Died in me forties. Outlived ya by twenty yar, Jack."

"What do you mean outlived me? I'm still alive."

"Right-o… as Jack." He gripped Jack's arm. "Yer me brother… Javier. Ya made this ol' salt wait a'most three hundred yar afore ya came back."

Jack sat up straighter in his seat. "Came back? Are you telling me that I'm your reincarnated brother?"

"Aye. Ya act and sound just like 'im." Alejandro smiled, displaying his chipped and rotted teeth.

The flight attendant returned with a tray holding two plastic cups with ice, a can of Coke, and two airline-sized bottles of rum. She placed the beverages in front of them and smiled. "That'll be fifteen dollars, please."

"Me treat, matey." Alejandro fished around in his vest pocket and pulled out a gold doubloon. He flipped it into the air with his thumb and landed it on the flight attendant's tray. "Keep th' change, me sweet."

She picked up the coin and held it up to the light, then turned and fixed her gaze on Alejandro. "Hmm, this looks like the real deal. My grandpa collected coins, so I know a thing or two. Wouldn't you rather pay with a credit card? This um, coin, or doubloon is worth too much."

"'Tis yers, missy. Just remember me fondly." He patted his chest. "Alejandro, th' greatest pirate ever ta sail th' Caribbean."

"Well ... okay. But, if you change your mind ..." The attendant walked away, turning around to stare at the pirate again. She pocketed the coin and moved to the back of the plane.

"Aren't you feeling generous," said Jack. "That coin is worth a helluva lot more than fifteen dollars."

"What's this ol' swashbuckler need money for? Me work here is done."

Jack poured the rum and Coke into his glass and hoisted it. "Cheers to my long-lost brother."

Alejandro opened the little bottle and knocked it back in one gulp. "Barely enough to wet me whistle."

"What happened to me, or Javier—back then?" asked Jack.

Alejandro paused, his jaw muscles twitching as if he were fighting down some strong emotion. "Ya lost a duel."

"What? You mean like a sword duel?"

"Aye. Defendin' th' love of yer life. Th' lovely Luisa Vega."

"What happened?"

"Th' dastardly Benito Mendoza, a beard-splitter o' th' lowest kind, a'ways had an eye fer Luisa. Connivin' bastard 'at he was, he'd hide an' watch as she took her morning walks. One day he nabbed her from behind, put a hand o'er her mouth, and dragged her inta th' woods. Lucky for Luisa, a hunter came by in th' nick o' time.

"As was th' custom back then, Javier challenged Benito to a duel to defend 'er honor. Th' next day, Benito ran his sword through me brother. One o' th' worst days of me life, th' other bein' Rose's passin'. Our *madre* died a yar later from pure grief." He gave a sad smile. "Me thinks ya were her favorite."

"Whatever happened to Benito?"

The pirate poked himself in his chest. "This ol' salt sent 'im to the bowels of hell wit' a rope around 'is neck. Th' next day me left Spain in th' starless dark night lookin' o'er me shoulder. Jumped a pirate ship and took to th' seas."

"This is why you wanted me to fall in love with Jessica, isn't it? You're giving me, or Javier, another chance for happiness."

The pirate nodded.

"Now I know why you said I was 'the one.'"

"Ye were me unfinished business. Jessica too. But—had to loosen ya up first... make ya see beyond yerself and yer boring world."

"Boring? That's a little strong, but I get your point."

"Th' circle is closed now. Rose's bloodline will be entwined with me own. Never had th' chance ta marry or have a family, and neither did Javier."

"So that means Jessica and I will have children?" asked Jack.

"Aye." The pirate winked. "Best ya hurry up and git married. That seed might a'ready be planted."

The prepare-to-land announcement squawking over the airplane's speakers woke Jack up with a start. It appeared he hadn't moved an inch. His legs were still stretched out on the empty seat next to him. Memories of his conversation with Alejandro flooded his head. Slightly panicked, he looked around for the shaggy pirate. *What the hell? Crazy dreams—they seemed so real. I must've slept like the dead.*

The flight attendant came down the aisle, checking to make sure everyone was seated and belted properly. "Um, excuse me, ma'am," said Jack, "did anyone sit next to me during the flight?"

"No, sir." She shook her head. "In fact, you slept the entire flight. Sorry—you missed the beverage and snack service."

Definitely a dream.

The plane touched down with a jerk. A quick glance out the window confirmed he was back in Michigan. Cloudy skies, and snow piled in dirty heaps along the runway. He shook his head to clear his muddled mind, pulled his phone from his pocket, and switched off airplane mode. The incoming texts and voicemails made his cell sound like a pinball machine.

Jack pulled his carry-on down from the overhead bin and grabbed his backpack. The pack felt especially hefty. A blast of frosty air hit him as he exited the plane and hurried down the jetway. His muscles tensed against the chill cutting through his lightweight jacket. He ignored the wintry assault and read the texts—all from Jessica.

I miss you!! Come back!
I think I saw your plane take off…
Can't stop thinking about you.
Did I mention I love you?
I'm picturing you naked right now.

A smiling devil face emoji punctuated the last sentence. He grinned and headed for the exit, happy to avoid the throng of people waiting for their luggage to appear on the carousel.

His phone pinged with another text from Jessica. This one included an attachment from the *Cayman Compass*, the island's newspaper. Curious, he opened the link. The headline read, "Historic Shuttered Inn for Sale." He scanned the article, realizing the abandoned inn near Spotts Public Beach was being sold by the government for $1. Only one stipulation—the inn had to be refurbished and put back into service.

Another text appeared on the phone's screen.

How would you like to own an inn? We'd make a great team.

Jack's heart skipped a beat. It had appeal. Being mildly handy, maybe he could do some of the refurb himself. He imagined a quaint inn, rather exclusive—a little restaurant inside. The idea revved him up. *Can't wait to talk to Jessica.*

Jack smiled to himself and ambled toward the airport's exit. He felt around in his backpack for the car keys. *What the…?* He stopped dead in his tracks and opened the zippered main compartment. His keys were there, buried in a pile of gold doubloons. An image flashed in his mind of Alejandro, flipping a coin to the flight attendant. *But that was a dream!*

The tone of his cell phone sounded. He tore his gaze from the coins and saw it was Jessica calling. He tapped 'accept.' "Hey there! I just landed."

"I thought you may have. I already miss you like mad. Did you get my texts?"

"Sure did." Jack picked up one of the doubloons and rubbed it between his thumb and index finger. "Let's buy that inn."

Jessica's happy squeal was so shrill he had to hold the phone away from his ear. "You mean that?" she asked.

"Absolutely."

"Wow. You surprise me. Do you think we can scrape together the money needed to fix the place up?"

"How 'bout we answer that question with a simple coin toss? Heads—full steam ahead; tails—no way."

"Go for it," said Jessica.

Jack flipped the doubloon in the air with his thumb, watched it tumble end-over-end, and caught it in his palm. He opened his hand. Heads. A whiff of pipe smoke wafted under his nose.

Acknowledgements

Nobody can write a book alone, and I'm so grateful to those who generously and happily contributed to this tale.

Many thanks to my early readers, Emily Anderson and Winifred Simpson, whose quality feedback sharpened the plot and enhanced the characters.

Dr. Daniel Webster, MD, provided medical expertise concerning injuries that took place in the story.

John Andrews, from the Royal Cayman Islands Police Force, willingly carved out time from his busy schedule to answer my many questions about the island's legal and criminal system. He graciously allowed me to use his name in the story.

Thanks to my early editor, Rama Devi. Her sharp eye and red pen saw me through the initial drafts of this book.

Special thanks to the talented Mission Point Press team who helped launch this book. Scott Couturier, a natural editor, has exceptional instincts for what makes a good yarn. His many suggestions, large and small, made my story better. You may indeed judge this book by its cover, thanks to Heather Shaw's design ideas and Mark Pate's artistic talents. Heather also was instrumental in the production and marketing of this novel. Doug Weaver provided his expertise in the art of managing the business of writing and publishing.

My husband read countless revisions of this tale. I looked to him for the male perspective of the story, and he offered helpful suggestions along the way. Like pointing out how Jack wouldn't give a rat's ass how many calories there are in a Mudslide. That's why that valuable bit of information is not in the book.

Grand Cayman Island is near and dear to my heart. Many of the locations and restaurants mentioned in the story are real. Some I had to make up for plot reasons. However, should you visit this beautiful place, don't pass up Seven Mile Beach or the Cayman Crystal Caves.

Eight years ago, I took a writing class from Aaron Stander. It changed my life. Thank you for your encouragement and friendship, then and now.

When she's not writing, you might find Marietta Hamady studying aquatic plant life on a Northern Michigan lake, or peering through binoculars at the resident baby eagle taking his first awkward flight. A travel enthusiast, Marietta got the idea for her first book by regularly visiting Grand Cayman, soaking up the island's sun and culture. No stranger to ghostly encounters, she enjoyed breathing life into a pirate ghost and sharing the beauty of a Caribbean island with her readers. You may email Marietta at: mariettaauthor@icloud.com. And, please stop by on Facebook: Marietta Hamady, Author. If you enjoyed this tale, please leave a review on Amazon—it'd be much appreciated.

Made in the USA
Monee, IL
23 September 2020

43187390R00132